Everything But The Skin

Radar DeBoard

UNCOMFORTABLY DARK HORROR

Book Cover Design and wrap by Don Noble of Rooster Republic

First edition 2025

Edited & formatted by 360 Editing, a division of Uncomfortably Dark Horror.

Editors: Candace Nola & Mort Stone

Published by Uncomfortably Dark Horror, owned and operated by Candace Nola. Pittsburgh, PA

Follow us on all social media, our Patreon, or on our website to stay up to date on new releases, appearances, and more!

Committed to *bringing you the best in horror, one uncomfortably dark page at a time.*

*Patreon*www.patreon.com/c/u12231330

Websitewww.uncomfortablydark.com

comes to making you feel pain. I want to read, and suffer, within his stories again and again."—Joseph Pesavento, author of HYDE COVE

CONTENTS

1

DRIVE THEM OUT

"Ten years we've waited; that's long enough. Now we take back what is ours."

"No."

"No?! Why?"

"We are too weak, and it's not right. We've had our vengeance. An eye was already taken for an eye."

"But our power is gone. It is missing, and we need it back."

"No, it is not ours anymore. That was the deal we made. Justice was delivered and the price we paid for it was our strength. Everything is balanced now, and it must stay that way."

"Wrong! We will die without it! That is not fair. That strength is ours, ours! No one else. And we were never after justice; it was always revenge. Retribution, just like those before us sought."

"I won't allow it. That's final!"

"You will starve soon. We will die. We need to eat."

"I can hold out. There's enough left for several weeks. It will be okay."

"No, no, no, I don't think so. You are a withered husk. We are wasting away. You know without flesh we will perish...and you are too much a coward to let that happen."

"I am not! How dare you! This won't work. I know your game. No, I will stand firm. You can't break me!"

"Do not fool yourself; you will break. You are weak. After all, a coward fears death and will bend to avoid it. With limbs that

can barely move and a stomach growling for relief, it will not be long."

"Why? Why do you want us to do this?"

"We must survive. We must live. Without flesh, we will die. You can feel that in your bones, in your skin, in your essence. This is how we survive. Give in. There is no shame in it, only survival."

"Fine. Fine! I...I relent."

"Excellent! Let us feast and regain our strength. We know what is needed and where to get it. Those who are not impure. Those not tainted with so much sin."

"No! We can't. They're children."

"And they have what rightfully belongs to us! We must take back what is ours. Plus...how tender their flesh is. How easily it peels off the bone."

"Not now; we don't have the strength. They are all together. There are too many of them. I will not murder them for nothing!"

"Then we must separate them. Drive them out of their sanctuary and pick them off like the delicious rats that they are."

"Okay...we'll do that. First, we'll do that. But then we wait. And when we strike, it will be only one of them. Maybe, and I do mean maybe, two at most."

"We shall see. Much can change after the first taste. The flesh is so delicate and delicious..."

"We can't kill any of them! Not until they have been separated, is that clear? We only scare them at first. Pull them apart, but no killing."

"Very well, have it your way. We will be humane to the little rodents. That should be easy enough. There are many ways to flush out vermin, but let's go with one we are well acquainted with: fire."

2

THE BURNING

1984

IT WAS THE SMOKE that woke Sophia. Not the desperate yells or sounds of frantic scrambling, but the distinct smell that stirred her. When she opened her eyes, there was a black fog already filling the room, making it difficult to breathe. An overwhelming mix of confusion and fear guided her actions as she pushed herself out of bed. Several of the other girls were already racing out of the room by the time she was on her feet and stumbling after them.

For some reason, even amidst all the chaos, her intuition told her to glance back toward where she had just been. In doing so, she spotted Angie still asleep in her bed. She wasted no time in turning back for her only friend as the smoke grew thicker with each passing second. A forceful cough was escaping her mouth every few seconds by the time she reached her sleeping compatriot. Even more alarming, she could see the flames climbing up from the floor below and licking the back wall of the room.

"Wake up!" she shrieked, shaking the unconscious girl. After that initially didn't work, she resorted to a well-placed slap across her friend's left cheek.

"Ow! What are you doing?" Angie yelled in a combination of shock and confusion as she sat up.

Sophia did not give a verbal response but instead grabbed her friend by the hand and yanked her out of bed. There were a few minor protests from Angie, but those quickly disappeared once the smoke brought on a hacking fit. The two raced out of the large sleeping quarters and into the long hallway, which led to the stairs down to the first floor. Thanks to the wood of the building being so weathered and worn, the flames were spreading at an alarming rate. Heat radiated from every inch of the area the two girls ran through.

As they descended the staircase, a flickering of sparks shot across their path and managed to land on their faces. Blinded by the sudden and intense heat, Sophia tripped on a step, which sent her tumbling down the staircase. Unfortunately, she was still holding tight to her friend's hand, and Angie was dragged behind her. The two girls violently descended until coming to an abrupt halt thanks to the wooden floor. Pain radiated from various spots all over their bodies, but they were not seriously injured. Though they were in agony, they managed to stumble to their feet after spending a minute or so recovering from the fall.

This momentary pause in their escape allowed the fire to catch up to them, and the flames had spread across the lobby. There was but fifty feet separating them from safety, and unfortunately, an inferno blocked most of that path. The odds did not look good for their survival, but Sophia would not allow that to slow her down. Demonstrating a surprising level of calmness given the situation and especially her age, she pushed the duo forward. There was still a path of sorts that remained untouched by the flames, and she navigated it while holding a tight grasp on her friend's hand. As they weaved their way through the danger, the fire grew ever closer, while the heat itself reached an unbearable intensity.

Just when the flames were only inches away from touching them, they reached the front doors. The metal knob was searing hot, but Sophia managed to hold on long enough to twist it. As she threw the door open, the duo raced down the cement steps and out into the night. The stars overhead looked beautiful and completely untouched by the chaos unfolding below. The two stared up at them for a moment until a series of approaching shouts snapped their attention away from the sky.

"Oh, girls! You're okay! Thank the heavens!" Sister Tamera exclaimed as she raced over to them. After embracing them in a hug, she quickly checked them over to make sure they were okay and let out an audible gasp when she noticed the large blisters forming on Sophia's right palm. "What happened to your hand?"

"I burned it on the door," Sophia replied. "It was really hot."

"I'm sure it was," Tamera commented as she glanced over each blister. They were enormous and had already taken up a quarter of her palm. She noticed that there were no yelps of pain or crying coming from the injured girl, and she inquired, "Doesn't it hurt?"

Sophia shook her head. "Not really. It itches though."

"Itches?" Sister Tamera repeated.

She wanted to continue asking her questions but was interrupted by her superior yelling, "Tamera, get those girls away from the building!"

Wordlessly, both girls were ushered into the congregation that had already formed a reasonable distance away from the dangerous inferno that was raging on. As she stood next to the large grouping of other girls who hated her, and she them, Sophia grimaced. She stared at the flames now engulfing parts of the outside of the orphanage and found them beautiful. Part of her preferred being next to the fire than the other girls. At least the inferno wouldn't call her such awful things.

"Hey," Angie said, poking Sophia and snapping her attention away from the burning building, "thanks for saving me."

"You're welcome," she replied, a small smile forming on her face. That small bit of gratitude left a nice, warm sensation in her chest. Sophia didn't ever experience nice feelings like that, so she wanted to hang on to it as long as possible. "That's what friends are for," Sophia added in a voice just above a whisper.

The two shared a glance as Angie responded, "I'm glad you're my friend."

Then the two went back to wordlessly staring at the fire in front of them. As they watched the flames dance in the night air, the nuns were busy talking among themselves. Sophia tried to tune them out, but eventually, she heard something that caught her attention as they continued to converse in low voices.

"I think someone might have started it."

"That's a bold thing to say. Is there any proof of that?"

"Maybe not proof, but something doesn't feel right. The fire spread way too quickly for it to have happened all on its own."

"Perhaps, but the building was falling apart anyway. With all that old wood in there, it was a tinderbox waiting to light at any moment."

"Well...that might very well be the case, but my gut tells me someone had a hand in it."

"Who would do such a thing? What motive could someone possibly have?"

"I can think of someone..."

"Don't you even say it," Sister Tamera suddenly snapped. "She is just a child," she lowered her voice even further to add, "and she was injured by the fire. There are blisters all over her hand."

Sophia wasn't stupid; she knew that one of the nuns was trying to accuse her of starting the fire. That nice, gentle feeling she had been experiencing was gone now. It had been replaced by hurt and shame. She wanted to run away. Far away from the nuns, so she couldn't hear them anymore, but there was nowhere to go. Plus, if she ran, it would only make her look guilty. So, she just stood there as they continued their conversation.

"A few blisters means nothing. That's such a minor injury she could have gotten on accident after she set the fire."

"Do you hear yourself?" Sister Tamera asked with disgust. "You are accusing a child, a *child*, of concocting this big master plan instead of realizing that this happened all on its own!"

She was suddenly interrupted by another nun asking, "Where's Father Marris?"

"I thought I saw him just a second ago."

"Is he not here?"

The sisters began speaking all at once, creating a cacophony of worried voices. This continued until a lone nun cut through the growing chatter by yelling in sudden horror, "Oh Lord! He must have still been inside!"

The commotion immediately escalated into a panic, as some of the nuns began running back toward the orphanage in a misguided attempt to rescue Marris. At the same time, several of the others were trying with all their might to stop the sisters from doing anything dangerous. This strange scene was playing out directly in front of Sophia and the other orphans. The other children seemed to be getting a tad antsy and worried due to what was occurring, but Sophia wasn't. She was enjoying watching the very people who had accused her of something so awful a few minutes prior, making utter fools of themselves. So, as the magnificent blaze raged on in the background, she took in the spectacle unfolding in front of her, not knowing when another opportunity like this would arise.

3

Unpleasant Living Arrangements

1984

A RANCID SMELL WAFTED into the air as the worn mop sloshed over the tile floor. The water used to clean the area was grey and murky. Though it contained cleaning agents, Sophia was sure the liquid wasn't helping. If anything, it was probably making the tile even dirtier, but that didn't matter to her. This wasn't her job. She was too young to have a job. Last time she checked, most nine-year-olds didn't have to mop floors, and yet, that's exactly what she was doing. All because her guardian was too lazy and too old to do his job correctly.

She hated the orphanage. At first, it seemed like a blessing when it burned down, but that notion turned out to be misguided. All the other orphans managed to find temporary housing or get permanently adopted. Every one of them, except for her. Though the nuns clearly hated her, they couldn't leave her all alone, since that would make them look bad. So, to keep up appearances, they found her a place to live. Of course, they also made sure that it would not be pleasant for her. Saint Sophia's Catholic School— that would be her home. It was a perfect fit for the church. After all, the local parish ran both the school and the orphanage. She already attended classes there, so why not live there? And as for a guardian? Well, the school janitor would do splendidly. He already lived on the grounds, so she would do so too. Truly, it was the best situation for all involved, except for her.

"Damn, girl. Are you almost done?" a shaky voice asked from down the hallway.

Sophia looked up from the puddle of dirty mop water she had just sloshed across a spot of tile and saw her appointed guardian shuffling along. The man was so ancient he needed to lean against the lockers a bit for support as he hobbled his way toward her. An audible sigh of annoyance escaped her lips as she dragged the weathered mop through the puddle of filthy water, then returned the wet cleaning implement to the bucket.

"I am now, Mr. Travers," she replied while holding back the anger burning inside her chest.

The elderly man let out a grunt as he responded, "Good, 'cause supper is ready. You'd better hurry, or I'm gonna eat your food."

An audible scoff escaped her lips as she watched the ancient janitor shamble back to his lair while she finished his job. Sophia let out a solitary groan, then began pushing the mop and bucket across the floor as they were too heavy for her to carry. It took a good five or six minutes of effort, but she made it to the supply closet where she dumped out the rancid liquid. From there, she headed to her left and took the staircase down into the basement. A few more turns through a couple of areas shrouded in shadow, and she finally entered a cluttered area that she unfortunately called home for the moment. She walked past the cabinets stacked with used paint cans and ended up in the only clear bit of space in the basement where her guardian sat, already chowing down.

"I couldn't wait any longer," he rudely explained with a mouthful of food. He chewed for a few seconds then swallowed. "If you want to eat with me, you're gonna have to get faster at mopping. My old stomach can't hold out all night waiting on ya," Travers explained as he wiped his lips on the left sleeve of his uniform.

Sophia ignored him and sat down on the other metal folding chair. The old piece of furniture creaked under her even though she was far under any reasonable weight limit that would normally put a strain on a proper chair. She reached down and picked up the bowl that was waiting for her on the floor, getting a whiff of what food awaited her. Baked beans, the same thing it always was. For the two months she had been living there, all but one of her meals had been the same damn thing. They were easy to make, and that's why they ate them every night. It only took a few minutes to warm them up in the newfangled microwave that Travers had been bribed with to take her. Part of her truly believed that machine was the only reason he agreed to be her guardian.

"You know..." Travers began and then stopped to hack up some phlegm in his throat. "Now that you're a little settled in and all, I think you should take on a little more responsibility."

She glanced up from stirring around the dinner in her lap and with surprise repeated, "More responsibility?"

The ancient man nodded. "Of course, you're almost ten, ain't ya? That's right around the time I started working at the cotton mill. Damn hard work, but it was honest. Made me appreciate the value of the dollar. You need some of that yourself."

"But...I'm already working," Sophia said in protest.

Travers dismissed her with a wave of his hand. "Oh, that's just mopping. That ain't the real work. Nah, maintenance, now that's the real work. You're gonna start helping me out on that. That way you'll start earning your keep around here."

"My keep? That's what mopping the floors was for!"

"Shoot, girl, that's just covering the cost of your dinner," the old janitor laughed. "You're livin' here rent-free, ain't ya? Plus, I paid for your school uniforms too. There's a lot you still gotta make up for, but don't you worry, you'll be earning your keep soon enough."

Sophia glanced behind her at the cot that Travers labeled as a bed, then down at her underwhelming meal. A glance upward gave her a view of a few flickering overhead lights and plenty of rusty, leaky pipes. This wasn't an existence worth working for;

she knew that. It was awful, and now she was being told it would be getting a little worse. That was her breaking point. For two months she had put up with it without a peep, but she couldn't anymore. A wave of grief slammed into her, and that powerful surge of emotion opened the waterworks. She couldn't hold back the tears as they rolled down her cheeks and dripped into her less than appealing supper.

"What on earth are you crying for?" the old man asked in genuine confusion.

"God hates me," she whimpered. "Everyone's always hated me. The other kids, the nuns...even you do. It's not fair! I didn't do anything to deserve this."

Travers stared at her for a long while, letting Sophia's weeping be the only noise. Finally, he said in a low but gentle voice, "I don't hate you, girl."

"You don't?"

He gave a small chuckle. "Of course I don't. You wouldn't be living with me if I did, now, would ya?" Travers glanced around the dismal space. "I know it ain't much, but it's all I've got. It's how I live, and I'm happy to share it with you."

Sophia's crying slowed down a bit and choked out, "T-Thank you."

"Now, why do you think everyone hates you?"

"Because they do," Sophia insisted. "They're so mean to me, calling me names and talking about me behind my back. I can feel it, their hate. It hurts. It hurts so much."

Travers slowly sat down his supper as he gave her his full attention. "Why do they treat ya' like that?"

"It's because I've been cursed."

"Cursed?"

"I...I've been marked...by a witch," she said, shame dripping from her voice.

"A witch? What on earth are you talking about?"

She gestured, "There's a mark on my back. The nuns, the nuns say it's the mark of a witch. They think...I'm a witch."

There was a long pause, and then Travers burst out laughing. "Oh shoot, girl, that's the craziest thing I ever did hear."

"Don't laugh at me!" Sophia snapped with a scowl etched on her face. "I'm serious."

It took a few seconds, but the laughter died down enough for the old man to respond, "I know you're being serious, but there ain't no such thing as witches. Them idiots don't know what they're talking about."

"It doesn't matter if they're wrong or not. They believe they're right, so they're mean to me." She covered her face with her hands. "Sometimes I think they're right. I do have a mark, and...it's really weird looking."

Travers let out a long sigh as he glanced up at the lone light in the room. He pondered what to say for a moment then asked, "Where's this big bad mark of yours?"

"It's on my back."

"Do you think I could see it? After all, I would like to know if I'm housing a witch," he said with a small but playful smile.

"I...I guess so," she hesitantly answered.

Sophia turned so her back was to the old man, then she lifted up the back of her shirt roughly halfway up her torso. Around the area near her left kidney sat the mark. It was dark purple with a shape very similar to a crescent moon. There was another shape just a few centimeters down from the first one that seemed to resemble a droplet of some sort. Travers leaned forward in his chair to get a slightly better look and hummed as he examined the spot from several feet away.

"The nuns...they say it's a moon with a blood drop coming from it," Sophia explained. "That's supposed to be a really important sign for witches."

Travers stroked his chin for a moment then slowly said, "Well...I hate to tell you this, girl...but that ain't no witch mark."

"It isn't?" she exclaimed as she whirled around to face him. "What is it then?"

He nonchalantly answered, "It's just a birthmark. Sure, the shape is interesting, but other than that, it's just a run-of-the-mill birthmark. So, you don't have to worry about anything."

"Yes, I do, because everyone still hates me."

"But I don't. I know it ain't much, but it's a start, right?"

"Sure...sure, it is."

Travers leaned back in his chair while crossing his arms. "And you don't have to worry about no witches either. They don't exist. None of that dumb, spooky, hokey stuff does."

"How are you so sure?"

"Because I was in WW2, and I saw a lot of bad things while I was there. A lot of very bad things which showed me that there ain't no monsters under the bed to be afraid of, because the real ones are walking around in the daylight. You see, in a world where people can do what I saw them do...there ain't no room for monsters, or ghosts, or witches."

"What...what did you see?"

"I...I can't talk about that. Not with you. Not yet, anyway." His gaze wandered off as memories from the war flashed through his mind. "Maybe someday..." he whispered. After a long and uncomfortable stretch of silence, he became aware of what he was doing and brought his attention back to Sophia. To change the subject, he said, "Tell you what. You help me out with more stuff around here, and I'll see about getting you an actual bed down here. A nice one too. Not like those stiff, uncomfortable ones I know they had you sleeping on at the orphanage. What do ya say?"

"I would like that," she replied with a weak smile. *At least it's a start,* she told herself.

4

THE FIRST SNACK

"THE TIME HAS COME."

"Wrong; we need to be patient."

"We have been patient! Eight months is patient enough. We are dying. There is no more time to wait."

"We can't, not tonight. We're far too weak."

"No, you are too weak. I am strong, and I will prove it."

"What are you doing? Stop! Quit moving! I told you to stop!"

"You do not order me! I, who kept you alive. I, who brought us back from near death. You will not kill us, not after all we've been through. Nothing will stop me."

"Please, don't do this!"

"Your whining won't change anything, you weakling."

"Don't! Stop! Please don't go any further. Please...I...no...wait! Wait, wait, just wait!"

"What! What do you want, you worm?"

"Fine. Fine, you win. We will do it. But with only one. One child and that's it."

"We only need one...for now. It's a good thing I have the perfect one already picked out."

"How...how did you? When did you find...why her?"

"Simple — she was the first one born. She has a sliver more of what's ours than the others. Once we eat her, we will be strong once more."

"No, we will survive. Nothing more. This is not to gain power. This is so we can live."

"If that is what you must tell yourself, then fine, but I will not lie. I am hungry. The thought of flesh makes my mouth water. Soon we will be feasting, and then our power will come back. After years with such weak flesh, we will be strong again. Now, let us begin."

"Wait! She cannot feel it. Not a single moment of pain. She is innocent. She does not deserve to experience such a terrible death."

"The child is sleeping. She will not wake up."

"You know what I mean. Even her essence must not be aware. No part of her, physical or spiritual, must be aware of what we do to her."

"Something like that can only be done with magic and power we cannot waste."

"Good thing we aren't wasting it then."

"It is foolish to make such a demand... "

"Either we cast the spell, or we starve. The choice is yours."

"Fine! Have it your way. Waste our precious energy. But know that it will only make me more ravenous. I will enjoy savoring every piece of meat from her bones, and they will all be raw."

5

PARTIALLY CORRECT AND PARTIALLY FRIENDS

1985

"Did you hear what happened to Taylor?" Sophia heard someone say a few lockers down from her. She tried to ignore the conversation and grab what she needed for her next class, but something immediately caught her attention.

"It's only been two days, right? You can't be missing if it's only been two days."

She peeked around her locker door to find out who was talking. Three of the most popular girls in the small-town school stood only a couple of feet away from her, making morbid speculations. Sophia knew she shouldn't eavesdrop, but her curiosity won out. She continued to peek around her locker as the trio spoke.

"She's not missing though, she's dead," Jenna, the leader of the group, said with confidence.

"How would you know that?" Aubrey, one of her lackeys, inquired.

Jenna leaned toward the other two, and Sophia poked her head out even further from her locker to hear better. The lead girl spoke in a voice barely above a whisper. "They found her skin in her bed."

"Who did?" Maria, the other toady, asked.

"Her fucking parents."

"Holy shit! No fucking way!" Aubry exclaimed.

Jenna spoke a little louder now, with some excitement in her voice. "I'm serious. Apparently, they went to wake her up and noticed she wasn't in bed, so they immediately called the cops. It wasn't until the police were searching the room that someone actually checked the bed. They pulled back the covers, and there it was. Her empty skin just lying there."

"What the hell does that mean?" Maria asked. "What do you mean it was just lying there? Just her skin?"

"Just her skin, nothing else. Someone broke in and skinned her alive," Jenna replied with a twisted grin of glee.

"Oh god, that's so fucked up!" Aubry exclaimed. "How the hell did her parents not hear that?"

Jenna shrugged. "Probably cause they're bad parents," she scoffed. "I mean, they couldn't even keep their own kid from running out into traffic. Adopting another one wasn't going to fix that problem."

"I bet it was the witch," Maria suddenly said, switching the subject.

Jenna rolled her eyes. "For the love of god, Shallowroot does not have a fucking witch. This town just sucks balls; that doesn't mean..."

Sophia wasn't expecting a pause, so she instinctively glanced in the direction of the gossiping girls, only to make eye contact with Jenna. Caught red-handed in the midst of eavesdropping... she froze like a deer in the headlights.

"Hey! You little fucking snoop," Jenna snapped as she stomped over to Sophia.

In a snap second judgment, Sophia decided to pretend like she wasn't aware of what was going on and turned her head so it would look as though she had been focused on something in her locker the whole time. The metal door was suddenly yanked from her grasp, and she turned to find Jenna's face only a few inches from hers.

"Did you like what you were hearing?"

"Huh? What are you talking about?" Sophia asked, playing dumb.

Jenna gave her a small shove as she snarled. "You were fucking eavesdropping, you little freak. I caught you staring, so don't try to deny it."

"No, I..." Sophia tried to protest, but another shove pushed her back a bit.

"Did you hear everything you wanted to? I bet you like that sort of thing, don't you, you freak?"

"I bet her and the janitor talk about that fucked-up stuff all the time," Aubry said, joining in the bullying.

Jenna laughed. "Oh, that's right! The creepy janitor is your adoptive daddy because no one else would take you. Probably because of that freaky birthmark on your back."

"Maybe she's in cahoots with the witch," Maria chimed in.

Instead of chastising her friend for such an outlandish comment, Jenna piggybacked off it. "Makes sense why she'd be so interested in poor Taylor being skinned alive." She pushed Sophia again. "I bet you had something to do with it, huh?"

"No! I wouldn't do anything like that," Sophia insisted as she took a step back. "I was just trying to get something out of my..."

"Cut the crap," Aubry interrupted, "and tell us how you did it."

"Yeah, where's the body?" Maria asked. "Is it out in the woods, or are you hiding her in the basement with your nasty dad?"

"Of course, we should have seen it, girls. Her and the janitor did it together. It all makes perfect sense now," Jenna laughed. "How did you two do it, hmm? Did you hold her down while he skinned her?"

"Stop! He would never do that. I would never do that," Sophia continued to insist. She wanted so desperately to punch Jenna, to cause some damage to her pretty little face, but that would only breed more hate for her. It would only give the popular girls what they wanted: more excuses to bully her. "I was just getting in my locker."

She turned her back on the trio and tried to run away from the situation, but something tripped her and she fell to the floor. The hard tile hurt as she slammed against it, ripples of pain coursing through her arms and legs. She let out an audible groan, then flipped onto her back to see that Jenna had stuck out her leg. That's what had tripped her.

"Oh, sorry about that," Jenna sneered sarcastically. "You know, for a psycho murderer, you really don't pay attention to your surroundings, do ya?" She lightly kicked at the girl already on the ground while adding, "You know, my mom told me that your creepy janitor had something to do with a missing woman about twenty years ago. They never found her body, but I'm sure that's because your buddy is so good at disposing of them. Just like you two did with Taylor."

"Where's your proof?" a new voice suddenly cut in.

Everyone's attention turned to see Angie staring down Jenna with a confident look on her face. Without saying a word, she held out a hand to Sophia, who took it and scrambled to her feet.

Jenna scoffed, "You keep helping out that freak, and people are going to start thinking you are one. It's never a good idea to hang out with murderers, you know that, right, Angie?"

"Where's your proof?" Angie asked once again, this time with a more forceful tone. She pushed forward until she was only a foot or so away from Jenna. "Did you see her do it? Because that's when you can accuse someone of something like that." When there wasn't an immediate response, she leaned in close and whispered, "Like...how I can accuse you of being a little bitch who pisses her pants because I saw you do it three years ago while we were at the orphanage."

A look of pure fury appeared in Jenna's eyes, and it seemed as though she was going to unleash a tirade on Angie. Then, her gaze turned to all the students gathered around them, and that anger quickly turned to worry. The girl was too vain, too engrossed with her popularity, to allow a secret like that to slip into the outside world. So, in a calculated move, she took a step back and stared down at Sophia in silence.

"Whatever. This little freak isn't worth my time," Jenna snapped.

She turned and walked away with her posse following right behind. Several moments passed with no one else moving, and then the group of students dispersed once they realized nothing else was going to happen.

"Thanks, I appreciate the help," Sophia said as she moved back over to her locker and shut it.

Angie smiled. "Of course, that's what friends are for."

"Are we?"

"What?"

"Are we still friends?" Sophia asked. "Since the orphanage burned down, we haven't talked. Not really."

The smile evaporated from Angie's face. "Yeah, I'm sorry. I've just been...getting adopted has been...a lot."

"Hmmm...yeah, I'm sure it has been. It must be really difficult living with the Martins," Sophia commented with resentment.

"Hey, don't get mad at me. I have nothing to do with what's happened to you."

"Yeah, but it still sucks," Sophia snapped. She let out a long sigh and then added in a meeker tone, "I could have really used a friend, but you weren't there."

Shame oozed from Angie's response. "I'm sorry. I guess I haven't been the best friend in the world, have I? It's just...things really have been crazy for me. I haven't settled in with the Martins yet, and it's just a lot...you know?" She placed a hand on Sophia's shoulder. "Once I get fully settled, I'll have you over, okay? We'll have a slumber party, and we can hang out and spend the whole night talking like we used to, but we won't have to whisper because I have a room all to myself. How does that sound?"

Sophia mumbled, "Pretty good, I guess."

"Oh shoot, we've gotta get to class. I'll talk to you later!"

Angie waved goodbye as she rushed off, leaving Sophia in an empty hallway. She doubted there would be a slumber party. All the things that had been said, were just to make Angie not feel so bad about abandoning her. There was no faith that they would even hang out again. Sophia even wondered if that interaction would be their last. The last time they would talk to each other as supposed friends. It was clear what was happening. Angie had gotten adopted and was moving on. She didn't need Sophia anymore. No one did. She felt so alone as she slunk off to her next class.

6

———

AN UNPLEASANT TALE

1985

AT FIRST, IT WAS only present around her feet and lower legs, but it quickly spread. Initially, it was a slightly uncomfortable heat, like what one would experience on a summer's day. After a few seconds, the temperature grew exponentially to the point where she could feel her skin bubble and burn. She screamed out in agony, in confusion, in terror, as the flames licked their way up her body. Sophia cried out for mercy, for any kind of help from the group of men huddled together in front of her, but they just stood there watching. As the fire rose to her neck, she wished for salvation and shrieked for rescue with all her might.

"Wake up, girl," a voice cut through the nightmare. "God dang girl, you gotta wake up."

She opened her eyes to find Travers staring down at her with worry and mild annoyance plastered across his face. Sophia sat up, and in confusion asked, "What...what happened?"

"You were screaming your lungs out, that's what happened," the old man replied as he moved back and sat down on his bed. "I thought you were being murdered with how loud you was. Damn, you got a set of pipes on you, that's for sure. Maybe you could join the church choir, I bet they'd pay ya."

"I'm sorry I woke you up."

"Again."

"Again," she repeated with a loud sigh.

Travers furrowed his brow as he asked, "What in the Sam hell is bugging you, girl? That's the second time this week you've been wailing away in your sleep, and it certainly isn't the first time this month."

"I've just been having nightmares, that's all," Sophia said, trying to downplay what was happening.

Ever since Taylor had gone missing, she had been having bad dreams. At first, it had only been once every week or so, and when she woke up, she couldn't remember what they had been about. But the nightmares had been coming much more frequently to where she had at least one a night. Even more disturbing, she remembered them perfectly. In fact, she could still smell the lingering odor of burning flesh in her nostrils, thanks to the latest one.

"Nightmares? What kind of nightmares?"

"You know, the usual kind. Stuff like falling off a building and spiders."

Travers eyed her skeptically. "I ain't ever known one of those kinds of dreams to leave someone screaming bloody murder in the middle of the night." He shook his head. "I know what you're dealing with, girl. Them are night terrors, and they certainly ain't fun."

Sophia scoffed, "Really? And why do you think that's what's happening to me?"

"Because when I first got back from the war, I had to deal with them every night. The damn things made me relive seeing my buddies get blown to bits and a whole hell of a lot of other terrible things I just wanted to forget." He locked eyes with her as he reiterated, "So I know what you're going through. You got a bad case of night terrors."

"Well, how did you deal with it? How did you make them go away?" Sophia placed her feet on the ground and focused on Travers, hoping to hear some magical cure to rid her of the nightmares.

"Who said I got rid of them? I'll still have one every year or so, but they did stop coming as often."

"So what, I just have to live with it? Is that what you're telling me?" Sophia asked with annoyance.

The old man shook his head. "No, that's not what I'm saying. When I got out of the war, I didn't have anybody. No one to talk to. I had to deal with it all by myself. It wasn't until a few years had passed that I ended up with a roommate who let me talk to them about the night terrors. That's when the damn things really decreased."

Sophia rolled her eyes. "Talk? That's going to take all this away? Just talking."

"It won't stop it, but it'll sure as hell help. Maybe you won't be screaming your lungs out every night. That alone makes it worth a shot."

She reflected on it for a moment. The last thing she wanted to do was talk about her nightmare, because she would have to recall it and drag the horrific scene to the front of her mind. However, she was desperate to find some relief from the terror-inducing barrages that plagued her unconscious mind.

"Okay," Sophia relented, "what am I supposed to do?"

Travers leaned back in his chair. "Shoot, girl, ain't it obvious? Just start talking. What have these night terrors been about?"

"Horrible things," she responded. A shudder ran down her spine as several horrific scenes flashed through her mind.

"What kind of horrific things?"

The first thing to flash through her mind were flames, but she pushed the thought of that nightmare away. It was too fresh to talk about just yet. "Something, I don't know what, but something, pushing its way out of a man."

Travers frowned. "That doesn't seem so bad. Why's that got you so worked up?"

"Because I always see the man start to bleed. The blood...it's everywhere, and that thing is just trying to get out of him. I never see what it is, but he dies, I know that. He dies, and then I wake up." She looked down at her hands as she tightly clasped them together in her lap. "I've had that one a couple of times now."

The old man nodded slowly. "I guess that would be a nasty thing to have to see over and over again." He stroked his chin. "So that's what's got you screaming at all hours of the night?"

She responded wordlessly by shaking her head.

He sighed. "Well, shoot, girl, if you don't talk about it, I can't help ya. The more you talk about it, the easier your life will be, I swear by it."

Sophia hesitated to respond, letting silence seep into the room. The two simply stared at each other until she sucked in a long breath, then gradually blew it out.

"Okay," she relented with a nod. "The night terror always starts the same way, with me being tied up by something. I don't know what it is though; I can't see it." Sophia paused, waiting for the old man to say something, but he just nodded for her to continue. "That's when the flames start, and the heat...the pain, it's so much. I-I can't fight it. The fire, it covers me and...and it hurts. I don't think I've ever felt that kind of pain. I...it's too much to handle. I can't handle it!" She had gotten so worked up explaining the dream that tears had formed at the corners of her eyes. There was nothing that could be done as one slid down her left cheek.

"You're okay, girl," Travers responded in a calm and reassuring voice. "It's just a dream. A messed up one for sure, but it ain't real. None of that pain is." He waited for her to relax a bit before continuing, "So...I take it this is the one that really gets to you. Hmmm, do you know why you getting burned like that?"

"N-no," she replied weakly, with a trembling voice.

"Sounds like some kind of witch trial or the like. You got witches on the mind?"

"Well...yeah, kind of."

He blinked a few times in surprise. "What on earth has got you thinking about that?"

"Taylor, the girl who disappeared a few months ago. They said she was skinned and that...and that a witch did it."

Travers scoffed, "Oh shoot, it weren't no witch. Probably a damn maniac, but it wasn't no witch that did that. There ain't no such thing, so you gotta stop thinking about it, girl. Otherwise, you'll keep having nightmares about the Salem witch trials or whatever other freaky stuff floatin' around inside your head."

Sophia took offense to the dismissive way the old man was treating her, and her tears immediately ceased. "That's stupid. How am I supposed to stop thinking about this stuff when I'm asleep?" She could tell that Travers was taken aback by her blunt response, so she added on to it, "And that nightmare isn't about the Salem witch trials. The men in it aren't dressed up as pilgrims."

Travers furrowed his brow at the last thing she said. "Men? You didn't say nothing about no men earlier. How many of them are there?"

She blinked a few times at the strange question, then pondered it for a moment. "I don't know, ten, maybe, or fifteen. I couldn't say."

"And they were wearing modern clothes?" he prodded.

Sophia replied, "Their clothes weren't new or anything, but they weren't ancient either. Maybe...maybe older people around town would wear them. And one of them looked like a priest. They were wearing the same kind of clothes that Father Marris used to wear."

Travers slumped in his chair as some of the color drained from his face. "How is that possible? That was fifteen years ago. She shouldn't know about that," he muttered to himself.

"Shouldn't know about what?"

The old man shot her an apprehensive look as he debated something in his mind. After a long silence, he let out a sigh and shook his head. As he folded his arms, he explained, "There was a lady, about fifteen years ago, give or take, who went missing. A bunch of folks say she just disappeared in the woods, got lost in all them trees, and never came out."

Sophia couldn't help but bluntly ask, "What does that have to do with anything?"

"Because someone started a rumor that she was a witch," he responded with a grim look. "You see, back then, some bad stuff was happening to the local farmers. Their cows were getting sick, and their crops kept dying no matter what they did. Despite us living in modern times, some people started to think that Shallowroot was cursed."

"Were we?"

"What's that?"

Sophia sat forward a bit, intrigued by the story as she inquired, "Was the town cursed?"

The old man laughed. "No, of course not. There's no such thing as curses. It took a couple of years for people to figure it out, but runoff from the steel factory had been seeping into the ground. Damn stuff almost destroyed every local farmer in the area."

"Steel factory? I didn't know Shallowroot had a steel factory."

"That's because it's been closed down for nearly a decade now. Shoot, I wouldn't expect a toddler to remember something like that," Travers replied as a sad expression appeared on his face. "Yup, that damn factory polluted our town, and those damn morons blamed an innocent woman for it. I don't think any of them actually thought she was a witch; they just wanted a scapegoat. Someone to take their anger out on."

Sophia raised an inquisitive eyebrow. "How do you know that people were blaming her?"

"Because some men at the steel factory said it themselves," the old man answered. "There was a group of them just spouting off the nonsense that she was behind everything. They were doing it for weeks, and then she went missing. Immediately after that, all the horseshit they had been spewing stopped. It wasn't a coincidence; anyone could see that. They did something to that poor woman."

"What happened to them?"

"Nothing," Travers answered with a sigh.

"What do you mean, nothing?" Sophia exclaimed in righteous fury. "They killed her! And no one did anything?"

The old man shrugged. "What could be done? There was no evidence to show they killed her. Hell, they never even found a body. Couldn't do a damn thing to these monsters, though I knew plenty of people who wanted to."

Sophia sat there in silence for a long while until she finally muttered, "That's not fair."

"I would figure you of all people would know by now that life isn't fair, and it ain't ever gonna change."

"So...you think my night terror has something to do with this..."

"Teresa. Teresa Stillwater. And yeah, I do. Like I said, they never found her body, or what happened to her for that matter. I ain't a superstitious kind of man, but maybe...maybe your nightmares are her way of communicating from somewhere else."

"Well, then why show that to me? I didn't know she even existed until just now. What am I supposed to do? How am I going to help her?"

"I'm not sure, but what I do know is that no good can come from acting on something like that. It ain't natural what's happening, and it's gotta stop."

Sophia was shocked at what she was hearing. "What? I can't just stop having dreams."

"Maybe not, but we can do our best to stop them from coming. I'm here for ya, girl. Any time you have a night terror, wake me up, and we'll sit here and talk through it. I've got a feeling that will help a lot. And whatever you do, don't go talking about this with other people."

"I...I don't understand. Why can't I talk to other people about this? They're just nightmares. You said it yourself, they're not real. So why can't I talk about them?"

Travers' calm tone turned to a commanding one in an instant. "Because I said so, that's why! I'm feeding you. I am clothing you and giving you a place to stay. As long as I am your guardian, you will do as I say, understand?"

Sophia was taken aback by the aggressiveness of the old man. He had never pulled this card with her before, and it left her a little confused. She didn't want to argue with him; she was too tired to do so. The nightmare had drained a lot from her, and the last thing she wanted to do was stay awake by getting into an argument. So, she did what any preteen would do; she lied to get the adult off her case.

"I won't talk to anyone about it," she replied in a dejected tone.

"Good," Travers nodded with a triumphant look on his face. "Now get some sleep."

7

——————

THEIR FAVORITE PARTS

"UGH, THAT'S DISGUSTING. WOULD you stop doing that?"

"What?"

"Eating like that, with your mouth open. You don't have to tear into it like a wild animal. What we're doing is already horrific enough. I don't need blood splattering everywhere too."

"But...the mess is what makes it fun. Besides the taste, it's my favorite part. Isn't it yours?"

"No."

"Then what's your favorite part?"

"None of it is! Not a damn thing! This is all out of necessity so we can live. If we didn't need to, I wouldn't do it. I hate this! I hate the whole damn thing!"

"I don't think so. In fact, I think you like it."

"Shut up and finish eating. I'm not in the mood for your games."

"I will...once you stop lying to yourself. Just because you were raised to believe that eating people is a big no-no, that doesn't mean you can't gain any pleasure from it."

"Except I don't, because it's disgusting."

"Then how come we've eaten three of the children so far? After all, you were so adamant about it only being one in the beginning."

"I...I underestimated how weak we really were. At the time I thought one would be enough."

"That's your excuse? You underestimated? How ridiculous that you continue to try and fool yourself into believing such nonsense! You might be able to lie to yourself, but not to me. I know you. I see the parts of you that you can't."

"I'm not like you!"

"And yet, here we are, still together. If I am such a monster, then why don't you just leave me to die? Or better yet, kill me yourself?"

"You know that's not possible. My...our...situation makes our separating impossible."

"True. You may be right on that point, but being so different from me? No, no, no. If that were the case, I wouldn't have to fight for a kidney each time."

"You don't have to fight for it. The only reason I go for the kidneys is because they're easier to eat. I need to eat a part of them, and that just happens to be..."

"It's the taste! The taste! The taste! The taste! I can see it on your face as you bite into it. There's the tiniest little smile that creeps up the corner of your lips. You like it! But instead of digging in, eating like me, you starve yourself! And for what? So, you don't offend anyone? So, no one else comes after you?"

"You're wrong. You're absolutely wrong. I don't enjoy any part of this!"

"Then starve! If you want to continue with your stupid morals, then go ahead and die...but you won't. You're too much of a coward. And the taste...it lingers in your mind. I can sense when you're thinking about it. That flesh is irresistible to you."

"What do you want from me? Why torment me like this? It doesn't help you if I admit that I like eating human flesh just as much as you. So why keep pushing it? What do you want?"

"I want more meat! More power! We are still too weak to achieve full retribution."

"We got our revenge over a decade ago. It's long past time to forgive and forget."

"No! There are still some that live who wronged us. They must perish, and so must this town. They forgot about us and buried our existence. For that, they must all die! And to kill them, we

need more strength. More flesh to eat, and we must spread more fear!"

"We have eaten more than enough for now. I won't allow you to go over another child. It's far too soon. We probably should have waited longer after the last one. Two months wasn't enough time. The smart thing to do now is wait."

"I'm tired of waiting! That's all we've done for over a decade. I'm sick of it! I want flesh, and I want it now!"

"No, and that is final! I don't want to take the life of another child, and it's too risky. What if someone gets suspicious and comes looking for us? We're too weak to fight off anyone right now. Patience — we must exercise patience. But there might be something we can still do that is helpful."

"Like what?"

"We need fear too; that way we can move about easier, and I think I have the best way to do that. We send a message."

"A message?"

"Yes, we let people know that we exist and that we're not to be trifled with. I believe you are more than capable of doing that, but I have one stipulation. No one can get hurt. You can do whatever terrifying and horrible thing comes to your mind, but it can't harm a single person. Understood?"

"Fine. If it means I can finally do something, I'll agree. That doesn't limit me too much. Plus, I have the perfect idea in mind for a message. Yes, this is going to be so much fun!"

8

A New Curfew

1985

SOPHIA TRIED TO BREAK out of line and head to the far end of the bleachers, but the second she took a step in that direction a teacher gestured for her to get back in line. She reluctantly did, as the girls in front of her slowly climbed up the steps and sat down in one of the rows. A knot of anxiety pulled in her gut as she realized that she would be sitting squarely in the middle of a row with people on either side of her. The last thing she wanted was to be surrounded by her classmates, who held nothing but contempt for her existence. Unfortunately, there was nothing she could do about it.

As she moved up the bleachers, she heard Jenna call out, "Look at the midget freak. She can't even climb stairs right!"

Jenna's lackeys cackled along with her as Sophia ignored them and moved past their row, relieved to find herself close to the top of the bleachers. Though it still wasn't ideal, at least there wouldn't be so many people behind her. She could always feel her classmates' eyes on the back of her head, and she welcomed the opportunity not to sense so many boring a hole into her skull. After a few more steps, she shimmied into the middle part of the row and took a seat. She stared straight ahead as the next student took the spot next to her.

"How are you doing?" a familiar voice asked.

Surprised to hear a somewhat friendly voice, she turned her gaze to the left and found that Angie was sitting right next to her. "Oh, you know, besides being called a freak everything is going absolutely fine," she sarcastically replied. "I feel like I could still use a friend, but I've made my peace with the fact that I don't have one."

"Come on, Soph, don't be like that."

"Don't," Sophia snapped. "You only talking to me every time someone goes missing in this town does not mean you can give me a nickname. It took almost a whole year for you to speak to me again, and of course, it just so happened to be right after Jason disappeared. Then, you don't so much as look in my direction for two months up until right now." She glared at her ex-best friend as she sarcastically said, "Hmmm...I wonder what happened recently that would make you want to talk to me."

"I..." Angie began to say but stopped herself. She placed her hands on her knees and squeezed them, then admitted, "Okay, it's true, I want to talk to you because Talia's gone missing, but it's only cause I'm worried about you."

Sophia scoffed, "It certainly doesn't seem like you do."

"I swear I do, it's just..."

"Just what?" Sophia cut her off. "You don't want to be seen with the freak? The undersized, underdeveloped freak who lives with the janitor. I get that. I would understand that if you just stopped lying to me and told me the truth."

"It's the Martins," Angie blurted out. When Sophia gave her a confused look, she explained, "The Martins don't want me hanging out with you. They say you're trouble. They...they forbid me from being around you outside of school. That's why I haven't talked to you much since I got adopted. I don't want to get kicked out. I'm scared of what will happen. I...I've got nowhere to go if that happens."

Sophia turned her focus forward and folded her arms. She sat there in silence, letting Angie squirm until she said, "That's not true. You can always bunk with me and old man Travers in the school's basement. We've got a spare supply closet that's way cozier than it looks."

The two burst out laughing as Angie replied, "Oh! I wonder why I didn't think of that."

That happy moment, surrounded by people who hated her, was the first good one Sophia had experienced in a while. Ever since telling him about her nightmares, the old man had been distant with her. She couldn't figure out what she had done to anger him, but it was hard to think straight with all the emotional pain weighing down on her. He had been the only one in so long who had cared about her, so it hurt more than anything that it seemed like she was losing him too. But that moment of camaraderie between her and Angie, though it was ever so fleeting, gave her some hope that things would be fine.

"All right, students!" Principal Mathers shouted, interrupting the bonding time the two girls were finally having. After a few seconds, it became clear that none of the children were stopping their conversations, so he raised his voice to a level close to a scream. "Quiet everyone!"

A hush fell over the auditorium as the leader of the school scanned the crowd with a stern look on his face. Though it was well hidden, Sophia could spot the tiniest bit of concern poking through his confident façade.

"As I'm sure most of you are aware, one of our very own went missing this week. This marks the second student who has disappeared so far this semester," Mathers began with a reserved tone. "In light of this situation, the city council has enacted a new stricter curfew of eight o'clock. This new ordinance will take effect immediately, and anyone caught out after this specified time will be detained and placed in police custody for their own good. Now, there are also several tips and tricks that can help keep you safe. The city council is circulating these throughout the community, but I wanted to go over them with you today." He took out a piece of paper and unfolded it, then sucked in a deep breath. "Number one..."

The doors of the gymnasium suddenly burst open as the gym teacher rushed inside. After a few steps, he stopped and stared at the students packing the bleachers. From his expression, he clearly hadn't known about the assembly. The obviously flustered man took a deep breath, then walked over to Mathers while maintaining a deliberately slow pace.

"What are you doing? Can't you see I'm in the middle of something?" Mathers said in an irritated but low voice.

"We, uh...they found Talia," the gym teacher whispered.

"What? Where?"

There was a moment of hesitation and then came a response that was covered in apprehension and fear: "Outside, well...what's left of her, anyway."

Mathers was about to ask a follow-up question when one of the students in the front row shouted, "They found Talia!"

"Now hold on, nothing has been confirmed!" the principal called out, trying to keep things calm.

One of the students leapt from their seat and shouted, "I have to see her!"

That launched a chain reaction as the others immediately bolted from their seats, driven by a morbid curiosity to see their classmate. Sophia and Angie went along with the crowd, while Mathers continued yelling for everyone to sit down. It was clear in his voice, though, that he had no way of punishing the children, not when all of them were disobeying. All the students poured out into the hallway and naturally headed for the front doors of the school. Since she was further toward the back of the crowd, Sophia heard screams of horror before seeing anything. Waves of panic swept over the crowd, mixing together shouts of terror with the sounds of overwhelmed crying. Somehow, the noises of at least a dozen people vomiting could be heard through the commotion.

"Oh my God! Who did this?"

"This is fucked up!"

"Someone get her down!"

The voices piqued her curiosity and pushed her to find out what was going on. Without even realizing it, Sophia found herself picking up her pace a bit in anticipation of what was waiting outside. As she exited the school, she noticed that everyone else was looking upward, so she turned her gaze in that direction. Instantly, she realized they were staring at the flagpole and the grotesque thing that had been hung from it. The flag had been ripped down, and in its place, Talia's body had been strung up. Except, it was too flat, too hollow looking to be her whole body. It was just her skin. Someone had taken the skin off a child and then hung it from a flagpole for the whole town to see, and it worked. Whoever they were, they had gotten everyone's attention.

9

———————

FAREWELL GUARDIAN

1985

HER SKIN, SHE COULD feel it peeling away from her body. Blood and tissue revealed itself as some invisible force pulled her epidermis off. She screamed, at least she tried to, but no sound came out. Somewhere in the horrifying process, Sophia's mind became cognizant that it was a nightmare. *It's not real,* she told herself, but the pain she was feeling gave her doubts. Regardless, she tried to convince herself to wake up, to break free from the terrible vision. Instead of her eyes suddenly flying open into consciousness, the ripping of her skin ceased as her point of view was catapulted somewhere else.

She was discombobulated for several seconds, but once she regained a bit of clarity, she found herself in someone else's point of view. Whoever she was seeing the world through in the strange dream of hers, they were progressing through a grouping of trees. Sophia simply observed in confusion as the mysterious person pushed on through the tree branches until coming into a clearing. That's when the stranger's gaze lifted from their feet to reveal they were at the backside of the middle school. A prickle of anxiety poked at her as the mysterious person moved closer to the brick building and began feeling their way along the wall.

Sophia didn't understand what was happening until the stranger came to a stop by a familiar window that was low to the ground. The person stooped down and peered inside, giving her a view of a cluttered area she was well acquainted with. Then the mysterious stranger pressed their hands against the glass of the window, giving her a chance to glimpse the appendages. She noticed that both hands were burnt, though the left one looked far more disfigured than the right. On top of that, the burns seemed to be old ones from years prior. She was far too focused on the hands themselves to notice that the appendages had started to push their way through the glass. The fingers pushed through the solid substance as easily as if they were being plunged into a stream of running water.

In astonishment, she noticed the rest of the stranger's body was simply phasing through the obstacle as well. In a matter of seconds, the mysterious person moved their body through solid matter and dropped down into the basement she called home. She continued to observe as the stranger pushed past things she saw on a daily basis. With a few steps, the unknown person moved into the open area of the basement where she and Travers slept, and that's when dread took hold. From the point of view she was observing through, she saw herself asleep, seemingly unaware of the intruder.

She could only watch as the two burnt hands extended down towards her unconscious body as pure terror gripped her gut. As the appendages drew within inches of her throat, she waited for them to inevitably begin to strangle her, but they didn't. Instead, the burnt fingers moved up to her face and dragged themselves over the surface of her skin. She wanted to gag at the sight but could only continue to helplessly watch what was unfolding. Eventually, the hands moved their attention up to her face and gently pried open her eyelids. The stranger's gaze lingered on her unmoving pupils for an excruciating amount of time.

Finally, the burnt fingers released their hold, and Sophia's eyelids closed while the unknown person's focus turned to the old man. In an instant, she could sense the malice that spilled from the intruder as they approached Travers. They were going to do something awful to him; she could feel it. Desperately, she tried to scream for the old man to wake up, but nothing happened. She was trapped inside of someone else's experience, and she could do nothing as they drew ever closer to her guardian. *It's only a dream,* she told herself, *nothing is going to happen. You'll wake up before anything bad happens.*

The stranger came to a stop directly over Travers and outstretched the less burnt of its two hands. Several moments passed with nothing happening, and then Sophia noticed something emerging from the unknown person's fingertips. A set of claws, almost like talons, pushed their way through the scarred tissue, reaching a length of at least two inches. The second the new feature had stopped growing, the hand moved with lightning-fast speed. She couldn't keep track of what had happened in the moment, but the aftermath revealed itself right away. A massive slit had been opened in Travers' neck. For a split-second, it seemed like nothing would come of it, then the blood started to pour from the open wound.

A sickening gurgling sound filled the air as Travers' eyes shot open. She could see the terror that filled his eyes but knew there was nothing that could be done. The old man tried to sit up, but the burnt hands pressed down on him, easily holding him in place. Rasping and wheezing noises continued to escape from the old janitor as he frantically struggled to breathe. Blood poured from the opening and spilled all over the bed. Travers began to choke on the blood as his features grew more desperate. Finally, after what seemed like an eternity, his struggle lessened until he stopped moving altogether. She witnessed the exact moment life left his eyes, and it sent a wave of despair coursing through her like she had never felt before.

The stranger continued to press down on the old man's corpse for another minute or so, then slowly removed its hand. She thought the nightmare was over. Travers was dead, and what more could be done, but she was wrong. The second hand, just as the first, began to grow a set of claws. Once both appendages had their weapons at the ready, the unknown person went to work. They tore into the already ripped-open neck, digging the claws into the flesh and pulling out chunks of it. This disgusting process continued until bone became visible. That's when the hands wrapped themselves around the body part and snapped it, the sound of breaking bone filling the air. From there, it only took a tug from the unnatural hands, and the skin was pulled clean from the corpse.

The hands eagerly scooped up their prize and held it so the stranger could gaze directly into the dead eyes of their kill. Sophia was overwhelmed by the surge of conflicting emotions swirling around inside her. There was disgust clashing against terror, while fury also bounced around, but more than anything, grief was prevalent. Travers didn't deserve this. He had been good to her; he was one of the few people who had. Now he was dead because of some monster, and for what? The man was a janitor, not some hardened criminal. She didn't believe that he had done anything to deserve something so horrific.

Regardless of what she believed though, he was still dead. The monster she had been forced to watch through had made sure of that. She desperately wanted to pull herself free from this point of view, but she was still trapped as the mysterious person turned their back on the carnage they had inflicted. They moved back through the clutter of the basement and back to the place they had come in through. As one of the gnarled hands began to phase through the solid structure like before, Sophia felt herself disconnecting from that reality. Everything went black, and she felt her consciousness being tugged back into her own body.

Suddenly, she felt in control and opened her eyes. She jolted upright in her bed, shaking from the ordeal she had just gone through. Sophia stared down at her hands while her mind tried to process everything. Her focus naturally moved to a red spot that was visible on the top of her right hand. She slowly flipped the appendage over so she could get a look at the back of it and found more of the crimson color splattered on it. Fear gripped her insides as she hesitantly turned her gaze toward Travers' bed. That's when she spotted the headless body lying there, and her suspicions were confirmed. It hadn't just been a nightmare. It'd really happened. Then, she did the only thing she could think to do; she screamed.

10

——————

HAD IT GONE TOO FAR?

"REVENGE! SWEET, SWEET REVENGE! Now, none of them live. They're all dead."

"That was too much."

"No, it wasn't. He harmed us. Over a decade without speaking out made him no better than the rest. His silence made him complicit. He hurt us, so he had to die. We did what was right."

"I wasn't talking about that part of it. Ripping his head off, parading it around like a trophy, that's going too far."

"I wanted a souvenir. At the very least we're owed that, especially since we couldn't take one from the others."

"You got what you wanted; now it's time for what I want."

"What is that supposed to mean?"

"I am tired. Now is the time we rest."

"Absolutely not! We just spread fear to all those insects; now is the time to strike! It would be stupid to stop now. We must keep going!"

"No! We've been doing what you want and nothing else for the past two years. It's exhausting, and I'm tired of fighting you. There will be no arguments. My word is final. We will sleep, go into hibernation. When we awake from that, then you can have a say in what we do."

"We need more flesh! Our strength is still out there; it has not been returned to us yet."

"There's plenty of power flowing through our veins for now. Also, the town is in full panic mode, and they will be hypervigilant for a while. Taking and eating another child now is not the right move. The fear alone is enough to survive off for years, so that is what we will do."

"I still want our power back. More of our flesh."

"Then you'll have to wait for some time. For the foreseeable future, we sleep. But in a few years, once we are fully awake, then perhaps we will take back more of what belongs to us."

11

——————

New Housing

1985

"Okay, here we are," Sister Tamera said as she gently pushed open the creaking door to her residence.

Sophia shuffled in after her, lingering in the doorway for a moment before fully coming inside. She scanned the living room, noticing the walls were adorned with various crucifixes and other Christian imagery. That was to be expected from a nun, but the sheer amount of it was a bit overwhelming to her. A lone couch sat against the far wall, while a single recliner occupied the area across from it. Besides those two pieces of furniture, nothing else was present in the area, so there was a bit of open space. The room itself was not large at all, and she easily spotted the entrance to the kitchen, which also seemed on the small side from what she could tell.

"Let me show you to your room."

Sophia didn't verbally respond and just followed behind the nun as they moved down the sole hallway in the home. Sister Tamera gently opened the door to a room on the left side of the corridor and smiled.

"Here we are," she said with a gentle but jovial tone. "This was my study until I moved everything out over the weekend, so it's a little barebones, but that's okay. You can fix it up however you like in due time." The two shared an awkward glance that lingered until Tamera broke it by saying, "Well, I'll let you get unpacked and settled. I'll be in the kitchen if you need anything."

"Thanks," Sophia muttered as the nun exited the room, leaving her alone.

She glanced around the barren room, which was completely empty except for the bed stuck in the middle of it. Sophia moved over to the lone piece of furniture and dropped her suitcase on the floor. She plopped down onto the mattress and let out a long, sorrowful sigh. Her emotions caught up with her as she stared ahead at nothing in particular. A tear rolled down her left cheek, and that opened the floodgates. She began weeping as memories of Travers flashed through her mind. For every flash of a happy moment, one of the old man's demise would accompany it.

"Do you prefer..." Sister Tamera asked as she suddenly entered the room. She took note of Sophia's state and stopped. "Oh, I'm so sorry. I um...I was just wondering what type of salad dressing you prefer."

Sophia continued to cry, but she brought her gaze up to meet the nun's. "Why am I cursed?"

"Cursed? Why do you say that?"

"Wherever I go, bad things happen to the people around me."

Sister Tamera thought about how to respond for a moment then asked, "Are you...thinking about what happened to Mr. Travers? Because that clearly wasn't your fault. The same tortured soul who's been kidnapping those poor children did it. What could you have done?"

"I could have done something!" Sophia suddenly yelled. Her frustration with herself poured out. "I slept through the whole thing! They tore his head off, and I did nothing. I could have screamed or...or fought them...but I just stayed asleep. The person who took care of me was murdered right next to me, and I didn't do a damn thing!"

"Maybe...maybe if you had woken up, you could have done something," Sister Tamera quietly said as she crossed over to the bed. She gently sat down next to Sophia as she continued, "But more likely than not you would have been killed too. And I think that would be the last thing that Mr. Travers would want. I can't imagine what you witnessed, or what you're going through, but I want you to know I'm here."

Sophia wiped some of her tears away as she shook her head. "Why? Why are you being so nice to me?"

"The Bible says to treat others as you would want to be treated."

"Oh, so it's just because of your religion," she replied in a defeated voice. "That makes sense."

Sister Tamera shook her head. "It's not just because of that, Sophia. I care about you. When you were at the orphanage, I could tell that you were an intelligent and caring little girl. No one else took the time to see that in you, but I did. You have the potential to do great things; I know you do. You just need an opportunity. I could think of nothing more fulfilling than helping you make something of yourself. So no, I'm not just being nice to you because my religion says I should. I'm being nice because I care about you, and I want you to do great things."

Sophia felt a surge of emotion flood her heart, and she reacted by throwing her arms around the nun. She wept even harder as she sobbed, "T-Thank you so m-much. C-can we j-just sit here for a bit?"

Sister Tamera gave a gentle smile. "Of course we can. We'll stay here as long as you need to."

12

A Discussion On Dreams

1989

THOUGH IT WAS INCREDIBLY mild, the mid-autumn breeze made Sophia shiver. It wasn't supposed to be this frigid, not so early into October, anyway. Her school uniform hadn't been made for such weather, but she didn't care enough to change it. Plus, for the first time in a while, she had found a secluded spot.

She wanted to be alone, at least for a little bit, to contemplate her dreams as of late. And since students had been dismissed for the day, the elementary school playground would remain empty. She meandered around the various equipment until taking a seat on one of the swings. The metal chains creaked as she gently rocked back and forth while her feet remained planted on the ground.

"I'd think you'd be too old for this place," Angie hollered as she approached her friend, a playful smile across her face.

"Well, I certainly look like I belong," she yelled back.

It was a diss on herself, and something she would have never had the confidence to do four years ago, but since the incident with Talia's skin being hung in front of their school, she and Angie had grown close. They were best friends, just like they had been when they were at the orphanage. Unfortunately, that didn't mean Sophia's social life was perfect.

Her appearance hadn't changed much since sixth grade, and because of that, she looked like an eleven-year-old instead of fifteen. This led to constant ridicule from her female class-mates, and the male ones avoiding her like the plague. It hurt her how young she looked, but she tried to hide how much it affected her with humor.

Angie pushed her way over the gravel. "You may look the part, but it doesn't mean you have to act it." She came to a stop right in front of her friend and asked, "Okay, so what's wrong?"

"Nothing," Sophia answered as she continued to rock back and forth. "Why do you think there is?"

With a long sigh, Angie sat down on the swing next to Sophia. "You didn't hang around after school. You never do that unless you want to be alone, and that's never a good thing. So, what happened?"

"Nothing," Sophia quickly responded. She glanced over at her friend and caught the disbelieving look in her eyes. She knew Angie would just keep pestering her, so she reluctantly decided to tell the truth. "Remember a couple years ago when a couple of our classmates went missing?"

Angie raised an inquisitive eyebrow, intrigued by the direction the conversation was going. "Yeah, how the hell could I forget? Especially after they found Talia's skin flopping in the breeze." She shuddered. "I still think about that all the time."

"Well, I was having dreams," Sophia began.

"Dreams?"

"I guess...they were actually nightmares. Really, really bad nightmares." Sophia shook her head. "The things that I was dreaming about...they were...terrifying. I can't describe it any other way."

"So...you had bad dreams a couple of years ago, and that's what's upsetting you right now?"

Sophia locked eyes with her friend. "Yes, because they were so awful. I couldn't sleep for weeks, and when I did, I would see something horrific. Those nightmares have haunted me."

"Soph, we've all had a nightmare or two. I had one a few nights ago. It's not worth getting worked up about," Angie said, trying to be helpful.

"You don't understand," Sophia insisted with annoyance. She took a deep breath then explained, "The last time I was having nightmares, I told old man Travers about it, and he acted really weird about the whole thing. He got distant after that, and a couple days later...that's when..."

"That's when he died," Angie realized with a gasp. "Oh, shit. Okay, now I can see why you're a little worried about it."

Sophia shook her head. "No, you really don't get it. The last time I started going through this shit, people went missing. Our classmates were skinned alive. Travers got his fucking head ripped off. But the second that all stopped happening...so did the nightmares."

"So, what, you think your dreams and that messed up stuff are related?"

"Honestly, yeah, I really do, and it scares me. I keep thinking that the person who did all those terrible things is back now. That they're going to do more, and the nightmares are a sign of that."

There was silence between the two of them as the autumn breeze gently wafted by. A few leaves fell to the ground somewhere behind them, and then Angie burst out laughing.

"Girl, we have got to get you out of Sister Tamera's house more. I know she's treating you nicely, but you're going crazy being couped up in there with nothing to do."

"I'm being serious," Sophia said with an angry scowl.

"Me too," Angie responded as she stood up from the swing. "Look, your nightmares are not some spooky thing trying to warn you about the future. They're nightmares and that's all. How long have you been having them?"

"A week or two."

"And has anything happened?" Angie inquired with a knowing tone.

Sophia shook her head. "No, no, nothing has happened."

Angie gestured with her hands. "See! If your nightmares were predicting the future, then something would have happened already. So, stop worrying about it. I'm sure it's not fun having them every night, but no one is going to get killed because of them. Don't get your panties in a wad."

It took her a few seconds, but Sophia finally relented to her friend's point of view. "I guess you're right, but I'm still having them. What am I supposed to do about that?"

"Would it help if you had someone there when you had one?"

Sophia shrugged. "I guess so. I honestly don't know."

"Then we'll give that a try," Angie replied with a smile. "I'll have you over for a sleepover this weekend."

"What about your parents? They don't want you around me," Sophia pointed out as she stood up.

Angie smirked. "I'm a high schooler now, so I've got more say in who I hang out with. They can pout all they want, but you're my best friend. As far as I'm concerned, you can stay over whenever you want."

Sophia smiled as a great deal of the anxiety she had been feeling melted away. As the autumn breeze picked up a bit, she said, "Thank you. I don't know what I would do without you sticking up for me."

13

A LONG REST OVER

"I DON'T LIKE IT. It takes too long to wake from the long sleep. My arms are still numb."

"No sense in complaining. It was needed to regain some of our strength and to draw attention away from us. No doubt the town has forgotten about us by now."

"Two weeks to walk is too long. It is too dangerous to be so helpless. Our enemies could have found us at any time."

"The risk was worth it. Surely you can feel that, the energy coursing through our veins. It hasn't been this strong in nearly twenty years. And we achieved it without ripping apart another child."

"But now we must have another one. We are starving. Death comes for us. If we do not eat the flesh soon, we will die!"

"You're right."

"I'm right? What game are you playing? You never agree with me."

"Even a broken clock is right twice a day."

"What?"

"Even you can be right every once in a while. Unfortunately, you happen to be right about this. More of our strength has returned thanks to the sleep, but it's not enough. We need food, as simple as that."

"Yes! Yes! There are still many left to choose from. Why not just get it out of the way? We'll sample a new child each day..."

"No! It will be one and only one. We are just killing the hunger. One should be enough to do that."

"We've been sleeping for so long, there's no way to know for sure. Why starve ourselves when we can feast?"

"Because it is the right thing to do. They are older now. They have lives of their own. Each of them is a fully-fledged person. To snuff out those lights just because we can will not end well. For them, and for us."

"Fine, fine, have it your way. It shall be one...for now. But you have given in to your hunger before, and this will be no different. Mark my words, we will feast soon enough, and when that happens, I will not save the kidneys for you."

14

UNWANTED ADVANCES

1969

TERESA PLACED THE FINAL file in the back folder and then gently closed the cabinet. It had taken well over her normal eight-hour shift, but she was done. Months of work on organizing the various files were finally complete, and she could celebrate. There was a slice of cake and a glass of milk with her name on it waiting at home. As she turned to leave the office, her mind focused on the sweet treat that awaited her, she was startled by the figure of someone standing in the doorway.

"Well, well, well, looks like I wasn't the only one staying late," Roy Taylor said as he took an exaggerated step into the office. "What's got you staying here at this hour of the night, my lovely lady?"

"I was just trying to finish up some filing," Teresa replied as she tried her best to hide her annoyance. She moved to exit the office, but Roy leaned against the doorway, blocking her path.

"Filing? I wouldn't think the boss was so gung-ho about getting something like that done so soon. After all, it's been piled up like that for years; it could have waited another day." He leaned forward and smirked, "I think there's another reason you're working so late."

She tried to keep from rolling her eyes as she responded, "No, that's really it. I just wanted to get it done and out of the way."

Teresa put a hand out to push past him as she added, "Speaking of getting out of the way..."

Roy suddenly snatched her wrist. "Now come on, you don't need to play coy. There's no one around." He yanked on her arm, forcefully pulling her closer to him. "I've seen the glances you've been shooting my way the past few weeks. I feel the same way too, baby."

Teresa pulled her head back in disgust as he leaned in for a kiss that was not going to be reciprocated. He closed his eyes and puckered his lips, which gave her an opening. She drove her knee right into his crotch, which sent an audible gasp of pain rocketing out from his mouth.

"You bitch!" he tried to shout, but due to him being doubled over in agony, it came out as a wheeze.

She tried to pull away from him as his left hand grasped for her neck. Thankfully, he didn't make contact with her, but Roy did manage to wrap some fingers around the necklace that was tucked inside her shirt. Teresa didn't notice this as she was desperately trying to get away from the man who clearly wanted to do unspeakable things to her. She pulled against him with all her might, and the chain of her necklace broke. While she stumbled backward, the hobbled man fell to the floor, clutching the necklace tightly in his hand. She tried to maneuver around him, but he made a desperate grab for her as she came within arm's length. Thankfully for her, she was able to hop back without getting caught.

"Let me through, Roy," she firmly ordered. It was a warning, though he didn't deserve one. She was giving him one last chance to end it there; otherwise, the violence would escalate.

He scoffed, "After you tried to take off my balls? I don't fucking think so!"

That was all the invitation she needed to deliver a swift kick to the man's face. A roar of anger came from Roy's lips as a speckling of blood flew from his busted nose.

"You bitch! I think you broke my nose."

She quickly maneuvered herself so that she was directly in front of his chest, then delivered a blow to his gut. "I'll do a hell of a lot more than that if you don't let me leave."

He sucked in a few lungfuls of air as he fumed over the fact he was getting walloped by a girl. Finally, Roy managed to sit up while cradling his testicles in one hand and still clutching the necklace in the other. He didn't want to relent, so instead he opened his palm and stared at the piece of jewelry. It was a piece of metal shaped into a symbol he had never seen before. It was three spirals that didn't touch one another, except in the center where they joined together in a small dot.

"What the hell is this?"

"Give that back," Teresa commanded as she leaned down to snatch it away.

Roy tried to grab her, but she was too swift and delivered a kick to his face.

"Agh! You piece of shit. You'll pay for this," he snarled, while holding up the necklace, "and your damn witchcraft isn't going to help you!"

Teresa administered another blow to his gut as she grunted, "I'm not a witch, I'm a Wiccan, but a Neanderthal like you wouldn't know the difference."

She spat on his face, then wordlessly left the room. Teresa waited until she was a few steps outside the doorway to book it across the metal walkway that led down to the factory floor. As she raced for her car, Roy sat on the floor leaning against a desk while trying to recover from the humiliating beating. He turned the necklace over and over in his hand as he promised himself that she would pay for this.

15

FIRST TIME

1989

ANXIETY BUBBLED IN HER gut as she reached out a hesitant hand to knock. She pulled it back for a moment to build up her courage, then actually went for it. As the sound of fingers hitting wood reached her ears, she felt as though she'd made a mistake. Part of Sophia wanted her to call it off, to turn around and just go home. However, before she could make a getaway, the door opened and a middle-aged woman stared at her with a look of confusion on her face.

"Hello, honey," the homeowner said in a gentle voice. "Are you lost? Do you need someone to call your parents?"

Sophia shook her head. "Uh...no, I'm not lost. I'm, uh, actually here to see Angie. I'm Sophia."

The soft demeanor of the woman hardened in an instant, and a judgmental scowl covered her face. "Huh, I thought you were supposed to be in the same grade as Angie."

"I am. I just look a lot younger than everyone else in my grade."

After a long pause, the woman stepped out of the way while keeping a firm grasp on her door handle. "I can see that," she muttered under her breath.

Sophia cautiously stepped inside, her suitcase tightly gripped in her hands. She took a glance at her surroundings as she took a few timid steps forward. The open living room had to be at least twice the size of Sister Tamera's, and there were far more personal possessions filling the extra space than she was accustomed to at her house. Her attention was drawn back to the entryway when the person she presumed was Mrs. Martin abruptly slammed the door shut.

"Try not to make too much noise tonight," Angie's mother said as she moved around Sophia. "And don't think you get free range of the kitchen or anything like that, so don't go in there snatching up treats that don't belong to you." She gave her guest a side-eye and added, "Don't even think about keeping my daughter up late; she has important things to do tomorrow. I want lights out by ten. Do I make myself clear?"

"Um, yes, ma'am," Sophia replied, trying to sound as respectful as possible.

"Mom! Why didn't you tell me Sophia was here?" Angie exclaimed with an annoyed tone as she entered the living room.

A loud sigh escaped from Mrs. Martin's mouth as she began heading toward the kitchen. As she moved, she called over her shoulder, "That's because she just got here." A few moments later, the older woman muttered to herself, "Have fun with that fucking freak."

Though she assumed she wasn't supposed to hear that, Sophia easily picked up on what was said about her and felt her self-confidence take a hit. Her classmates called her much worse things on a near daily basis, but hearing something hurtful like that from an adult landed way harder.

"Well, come on. Let's go to my room," Angie said with a cheerful smile.

Before Sophia could protest, her friend grabbed her hand and eagerly hustled down the hallway. She allowed herself to be pulled along but had made up her mind that she wasn't going to stay. The rest of the house clearly didn't want her there, and she didn't feel like she could deal with that kind of animosity directed at her for the whole night. Angie led her across the doorway into her bedroom while grabbing hold of the doorknob in the process. Mere seconds after they had crossed the threshold, the door was shut tight.

"Listen, I don't think…"

"I'm sorry about my mom being a bitch to you," Angie cut in.

Clearly, she wouldn't be accepting excuses, but Sophia gave it a try, anyway. "She doesn't want me here, and I'm sure the rest of your family doesn't either. I-I don't think I should stay the night."

"Forget about them. I want you to stay; that's all that matters. Plus, you don't have to talk to them; we could stay in here for the rest of the night."

Sophia shook her head. "It matters to me. You're one of the only people in this backwater town who doesn't treat me like some kind of sickness. You don't even make fun of me for looking like a child compared to everyone else."

"I think you look cute. It makes you different from all the other wannabe cheerleader types in this town. Besides, you don't look like a child. A little younger, sure, but that's just part of your charm," Angie said with a light smile.

"Thanks," Sophia replied with a tinge of annoyance. The compliments had successfully knocked the course of her argument off track, and now she needed a moment to reorient herself for what to say next. It took a moment, but she finally continued, "The point is, I feel like a freak every second of my life when I'm not with you or Sister Tamera. I don't want to spend any more of my time feeling like a disease if I don't have to."

As she turned and stepped toward the door, Angie scooted in her path, blocking the way. "You're not a freak though. If everyone else in this town took the time, they would find out that you're a kind, wonderful, and beautiful person."

"But they won't. They never will," Sophia objected. She shook her head. "Angie, being an outcast is my life. I can accept that. But I'm also not going to feel like one just to hang out." She gestured for her friend to get out of the way. "I'm leaving."

"Come on, don't go. We'll have fun tonight. I promise."

"You can't promise that, and I don't want to spend the night locked inside your room like an animal."

"What can I say that will make you stay?"

"Nothing," Sophia firmly replied as annoyance flared in her tone.

"Then..." Angie hesitated as light hue of red began to appear on her cheeks, "what if I did something instead?"

"What?"

In an instant, Angie closed the gap between the two of them so that their faces were mere inches away from each other. Before Sophia could even react, her friend had placed a gentle hand against her left cheek. Only a second more passed, and then Angie leaned in and kissed her. The gesture only lasted for a few moments, but it was enough to make Sophia's mind go totally blank.

She didn't know how to react to the situation, so she just stood there. Her focus was so wrapped up in what new thing was occurring in front of her that she didn't place any attention on the suitcase that was still in her grasp. The luggage slipped from her fingers and fell to the floor with a thump, startling both girls, which in turn ended the experience.

"Oh...I uh..." Sophia instinctively began to talk, but her mind hadn't recovered from the surprising interaction, so no other words came out.

An expression of hurt crossed Angie's face as she lowered her gaze. "You don't feel the same."

"It's not that..."

"No, I get it. I mean, you know, it's wild even to think that something like that is possible," she scoffed at herself more than anything else. "Girls don't like girls. That's not possible. I mean, who ever heard of something like that? It's just ridiculous..."

Now it was Sophia's turn to reassure Angie as she reached out and took her friend's hand in hers. "That was my first kiss." She slowly smiled as she added, "And I don't think it'll be my last."

The two kissed once more, pulling closer to each other. That second one led to another, then another, going on for enough time that they became comfortable enough to press together. This came to an abrupt end with a loud knock on Angie's door. Reflexively, the two pulled away from each other just as Mrs. Martin's voice called out, "What are you two doing in there?"

"Just talking, Mom," Angie quickly replied.

"Then how come you're doing it so quietly?" her mother inquired, with suspicion oozing from her voice.

"Because we don't know if anyone is eavesdropping on us," Angie retorted.

There came a long pause, and then her mother simply replied with, "Oh."

This response was followed by the sound of footsteps moving down the hallway away from the bedroom. The two waited for the noises to grow distant enough, then they shared a laugh.

"Seems my mom is a bit of a snoop," Angie giggled.

"Clearly," Sophia agreed with a chuckle. After a few moments, her laughter died down, and she added, "Maybe...we should play it safe then. Just in case someone else starts getting nosy."

There was some reluctance as Angie nodded. "Yeah, you're probably right." Suddenly she perked up as she realized something. "Does this mean you're staying?"

"Yeah, I guess so."

"It looks like my little gamble paid off," Angie said with a smile. She leaned toward Sophia's ear and whispered, "In more ways than one."

Sophia couldn't help but laugh at that as the two settled in for a night spent together as just friends. Though the kisses continued to linger in her mind throughout the night. She couldn't help replaying each one dozens of times in her mind. They felt good, and not just in a physical sense. It made her feel wanted, a true rarity for her. The experience of another person wanting her was new and exhilarating, and she welcomed it with open arms. It gave her comfort, which helped ease her to sleep several hours later.

However, the comfort was short-lived as another nightmare played itself out in her mind. Just like the time she'd witnessed Travers' demise, she found herself watching through someone else's eyes as they snuck around in the dark. Sophia couldn't identify where the killer was prowling around, but she could see that it was some type of residential area. Very quickly, the mysterious person honed in on a particular house and moved over to the left side of it. From there, they phased their way through an outside window, allowing them to enter a small bedroom.

Everything was bathed in darkness, so it made it difficult to identify anything, but by the time the dangerous stranger had produced talons from their fingertips, she knew who was sleeping soundly in the bed. Jenna, her main antagonist, the one who had brought so much pain to her life, was on the proverbial chopping block. Part of Sophia eagerly wanted to see her bleed, but any notion of that disappeared the moment a talon slid across her bully's throat. As crimson poured from the gash, Jenna's body jerked in the bed for a moment before the stranger pressed their weight down on it. Then, Sophia had the misfortune of witnessing the killer use their claws to peel skin away from flesh and muscle. She wasn't able to pull herself out of the nightmare until the stranger leaned down to take the first bite of raw meat.

16

STOKING A WITCH HUNT

1969

"I JUST CAN'T UNDERSTAND it," the frustrated steelworker began as he plopped down on the wooden bench.

Travers tried not to pay attention to the conversation and focused on getting packed up for the day, but the proximity made it nearly impossible to tune it out completely.

"Four years I've been doing part-time work on that farm, and I ain't never seen things get as bad as this," the disgruntled man continued as he untied one of his work boots.

His coworker shrugged. "Maybe the old man overdid it this year on the crops."

"No, that's not it. That would account for some of his stuff dying off, but the whole damn field? No way."

Travers was about to stand up and head out when he spotted Roy sauntering over out of the corner of his eye. On good days he could barely stand the words coming out of the obnoxious prick's mouth and today was not one of those. He knew that if his coworker started spouting off to him (like he tended to do), he might very well go off and deck him.

The last thing he wanted was a fight, so he decided to remain seated with his gaze locked on some random spot in front of him. His hope was that Roy wouldn't pay any attention to him and that he could slip out of the crowded locker room with ease. Sure enough, the biggest douche in the steel mill sauntered right on past him and over to the coworkers still chatting about failing crops.

"I know what's causing the crops to die out," Roy interjected.

The initial man who had been complaining had a skeptical look on his face as he responded, "Oh really? And what might that be?"

Roy leaned in close, and with a voice that was well above a whisper, yet pretended to be one, said, "A witch."

"What? What the hell did you just say?" one of the men asked in bewilderment.

Roy wasted no time in repeating, "I said, a witch. That's what's doing it."

There was a tense moment of silence that hung in the air, which convinced Travers to turn his attention to the interaction. He tried to read the expressions of the two coworkers sitting on the bench, but he couldn't get a good idea of what they were thinking. In his mind, he desperately hoped that kind of stupid comment would be the final straw and that one of them would beat the snot out of Roy, so he didn't have to. Finally, a response to the outlandish claim came in the form of rapturous laughter.

"That's the dumbest thing I've ever heard!" the coworker who had started the whole conversation cried out in between his laughter. "A witch! How the hell did you come up with something so stupid?"

Roy answered the question by reaching into his pocket and pulling something out. It took a moment for Travers to identify that he had brought out a necklace with a strange symbol connected with a chain.

"What's that? You got a piece of jewelry for us?" the other man joked.

"It's a witch's symbol," Roy said in a very serious voice. "No doubt it's been used to summon something evil and not from our world."

Another man joined in the conversation by riffing, "Or it's just a necklace."

As another round of laughter kicked off, a look of anger crept across Roy's face. "Tell that to the cows dying in the fields." That was enough to shut everyone up. "Or how about the other live-stock that's just keeling over left and right? That ain't natural."

With a quick survey of the room, it became clear that the others were drifting toward the conversation. Travers had a bad feeling about the situation. Since there were no longer jeers and laughter at Roy's ridiculous theory, it meant they were starting to come around to it. He needed to say something to stop the dangerous idea's momentum.

"That's ridiculous!" he proclaimed as he got to his feet.

"Why? Because you don't want to accept the truth?" Roy responded with a cocky grin.

Travers scoffed to hide his growing worry. "No, because it's the twentieth century and not Salem, Mass three hundred years ago. There's no such thing as witches."

"Then what about the crops and the animals dying off, hmm?" Roy prodded. "What's your explanation for that?"

"I...I don't have one," Travers reluctantly admitted. He wasted no time in adding, "But I haven't taken the time to go inspecting all the dead cows around Shallowroot to find out." A quick glance at his coworkers showed they didn't have much confidence in his answer. In an attempt to throw some doubt Roy's way, he asked, "How do we know that necklace belongs to a witch? After all, I don't know any witches in Shallowroot, so who does it supposedly belong to?"

"Teresa Stillwater," Roy replied with confidence.

There was a little too much confidence in the response, and it gave Travers the opening he was looking for. "And how the hell did you get that necklace from Teresa? I'm pretty damn sure she didn't just give it to ya."

"I found her last week using it to perform spells. It took everything I had, but I managed to stop her just in the nick of time."

"Hmmm...how strange," Travers said as he stepped closer to Roy. "It just so happens that the woman you've been lusting after since she started here, who won't give you the time of day, happens to be a witch." He got right in the false accuser's face as he continued, "That's convenient. Hell, even more convenient is that you, and just you, managed to stumble across her doing something evil. That sounds like a big load of bullshit to me."

The sound of unsure murmurs began to make their way throughout the locker room, and Travers felt that would be enough for now. Roy's true motives had been laid bare; the others wouldn't be falling for his tricks again anytime soon. There was too much doubt for anyone to believe such claims, and that would suffice for now.

As he turned to head out of the locker room, Travers called out so all could hear him, "I'm heading home now. I've worked too damn hard today to let some snake oil salesman try to sell me his lies." He glanced over his shoulder at the group of his coworkers. "I imagine the rest of ya feel the same way."

17

STILL HUNGRY

"HOW CAN THIS BE? It's only been a couple of days; we shouldn't be hungry."

"We never stopped being hungry! That girl wasn't enough. Not after a long sleep. We need more. At least two more!"

"One. I will give you one, but that's it."

"Interesting...I was expecting a fight. Why suddenly do you give so easily?"

"My stomach cries in pain. Clearly, we need to eat more. I don't like it. In fact, I want to throw up just thinking about it, but it's for our survival."

"And are you sure one will be enough? Our bellies are growling for flesh. I think a single child will not nearly be enough."

"They are not children anymore. We have slept so long that they have grown beyond that. Now they are larger and stronger. After our last meal, I could sense more power flowing back into us than ever before. I am relenting on one, but not on two."

"Very well, but when your stomach starts growling in the night, do not come crying to me."

"There will be no whining. I've never done it before, and I shall not start now. Not when my conscience is clean."

"I didn't think someone who snacked on raw kidneys could have a clean conscience."

"Well, I do. I have to, otherwise, I can't sleep at night. And if that happens for too long, we both won't survive."

18

CALM BEFORE THE STORM

1989

"Hey! I stopped by your place yesterday, but Sister Tamera said you were out," Angie said as she came to a stop next to Sophia's open locker door.

"Uh...yeah, I'm sure I was taking a walk in the woods."

Angie leaned in and whispered, "If I didn't know any better, I would say you were avoiding me." She chuckled, but when no visible response came from her friend, her smile vanished. "Y-You're not avoiding me, right?"

"No. No, I'm definitely not avoiding you," Sophia replied as she continued to place her full attention on rooting around in her locker.

"Well, it seems like that's exactly what you're doing."

Angie reached out and touched her girlfriend's left hand, which was placed just outside of the locker. Instinctively, Sophia ripped her hand away. That finally got her to turn her gaze away from the locker, and she was greeted by a look of hurt. Immediately feeling regret for the knee-jerk reaction she had committed, she let out a sigh that was weighed down with so much emotion.

"I'm not trying to avoid you." Sophia glanced around to make sure no one was listening and then whispered, "What we did on Friday...that made me the happiest I've been in a long, long time."

"Then why are you trying to pretend like it didn't happen?"

Sophia shook her head. "I'm not. It's not you. It's something else." She hesitated and then admitted, "Friday night, I had one of those nightmares. I saw...I saw someone kill Jenna." There was a long pause as she put her lips only a few inches away from Angie's ear. "Jenna is dead."

"You don't know that," Angie replied dismissively.

"I know it," Sophia insisted. "I know it because I saw it."

"How come we haven't heard about it then?"

"After what happened a few years ago, you and I both know that no one wants something like that to happen again. They're keeping it under wraps for now until they have no other choice."

Angie raised an inquisitive eyebrow. "And when would that be?"

"When they find her body...what's left of it, anyway." She noticed that her friend still had a skeptical look sprawled across her face, so she added, "You haven't seen her today, have you? Her minions are here, roaming the halls like the rats they are, but she isn't."

Angie sighed, "That doesn't mean she's dead. She could be sick or running late."

Sophia locked eyes with her friend turned lover as she took hold of her hand. "But she isn't. That person...that thing got to her and killed her."

The look was finally enough to wear Angie down, and she relented with a loud sigh. "Okay, I believe you. But...what does this mean?"

"It means a murderer is back on the loose."

"We'll be okay though, right?" Angie asked out loud, more to convince herself than anything.

Sophia slowly shook her head. "I don't think so. Something is different this time."

"Different? Different how?"

She squeezed her girlfriend's hand as she explained, "They feel...hungry. More animal-like than before. There's a viciousness that's seeping into the air, and I don't like it one bit."

"So, what should we do about it?" Angie inquired as a group of girls pushed by.

Sophia lowered her voice so none of the passing group could hear. "Stay safe. Sticking together at all hours is probably our best bet."

"What about at night? We can't have a slumber party all the time. Especially not on school nights."

"I guess you're right," Sophia mumbled as she thought it over. "Just stay alert then. Keep watch for anything suspicious at night."

"How do you expect me to do that? Not sleeping?" She noticed the look on her girlfriend's face and scoffed, "You're serious?"

"It's just until the weekend, then I can be with you and keep you safe." Sophia squeezed Angie's hand. "I can't lose you. I don't know what I would do if I did."

19

Too Late

1969

THE CAR WAS NOT built to handle the gravel road, and the erratic driving did nothing to help. Travers wiped off a bit of sweat that had formed on his forehead while his eyes furiously searched the landscape. He noticed the turnoff mere seconds before he would have missed it, so, reacting in the heat of the moment, he sharply yanked the steering wheel. The tires skidded over the dirt as the car struggled to right itself. Thankfully, the worn vehicle held out and successfully progressed onto the new road. He continued to speed through the new area for several minutes until coming to a small open field that ended in a large swath of trees.

Travers wasted no time in exiting the car and booking it toward the woods. The autumn weather had done its work, and the trees were stripped bare. Leaves covered the ground and crunched under his feet as he pushed through the densely wooded area. Branches slapped against his skin and poked him as he progressed, but it did not deter him. Truthfully, he had absolutely no idea where he needed to go. All he knew was that someone needed help, and he silently prayed that he would make it in time. He was not a religious man, so he prayed to the universe, to the rocks, to the dead trees, to anything that would listen to him.

"Please don't let me be late. Let me make it there in time."

His gaze eventually drifted to the sky in search of some identifying symbol or sign that would give him a sense of where to go. As he scanned the area above the trees, he picked up on a plume of smoke coming from somewhere off to his right. It wasn't heavy. In fact, the color of the smoke itself was on the lighter side. Perhaps things had just started. Maybe no one had been truly hurt yet. He clung to that hope and took off in the direction of the plume. All the while, sweat freely dripped down his cheeks as the exertion wore him down with each step. By the time he stumbled into the first clearing he came across, his lungs were burning while his legs screamed from overexertion.

A quick scan told him that he had located where the smoke was coming from, but oddly enough, no one was there. He had expected a crowd of his coworkers, enough of them to form a small mob at least. Instead, there was only one person, down on their knees silently praying. The lone individual didn't react as Travers stumbled over to them. It wasn't until he placed a hand on their shoulder that the person glanced up at him, horror filling his expression. Though he wasn't a churchgoer himself, he recognized the priestly garb that the individual was adorned in and from that was able to identify who they were.

"Father, what are you doing here?" When he was met with incoherent praying, he bent down to be at eye level with Father Marris. "Where is everyone? What happened?"

Marris didn't verbally respond, but his eyes did move, briefly glancing at something in their peripheral. Travers turned his attention in that direction and came to rest on the spot where smoke continued to rise from. He hadn't taken much time to look at it until then, but a disturbing detail became apparent to him. Amid the burnt patch of earth was a large shape, a blackened mass that was separate from the dirt. He took his time standing up and shambling over to the spot as dread squeezed at his gut. By the time he was standing before the mass, he knew exactly what it was. A body burnt beyond recognition, reaching a point where the limbs were barely discernible from the rest of it.

"My God, what have you done?" Travers whispered with a shaking voice.

"It was not me. I did not do this. They did. It was supposed to be an exorcism. She was possessed. They told me she was possessed. I was only thinking of her mortal soul. Even after they started to...I only wanted to help her." Marris felt like he had to speak up in his defense.

This set off a spark of rage in Travers, and he responded with a guttural shriek. "You didn't do anything?" he screamed as he stomped over to the Father. He grabbed him by his collar. "You let her die!"

"What was I supposed to do? There were over a dozen of them. They would have killed me too."

Travers scoffed then pushed the man to the ground. "I thought your type wanted to die so you could get to heaven faster."

Marris stared up at the enraged man, trembling with fear. Regardless, he decided to still open his mouth. "She was a witch."

"What?"

"She was a witch. I heard her confess it. S-She prayed to demons, to Satan for deliverance. All the rumors were true."

"For fuck's sake, I'd be praying to anything to come save me if I was being set on fire!" Travers yelled into the cowering man's face. "Besides," he continued in a softer voice, "she didn't deserve this. No one deserves this."

"She was a devil worshiper. She had to pay for her sins."

"Says who?" Travers snapped. "You? Your god? That collection of cow-fucking morons?" He brought his fist back as if he was going to throw a punch but stopped short. "No one has earned the right to decide that. No one. No one gets to be judge, jury, and executioner, but you let them get away with it."

"I couldn't have done anything. They would have killed me too," Marris insisted.

Travers gazed at the pitiful man before him and sneered, "You're a coward. You'll always be a coward. I hope you live with that for the rest of your life. Every night I hope you wake up screaming because you stood by and let this happen. I hope you never get another good night's rest until the day you die." He made his way back to the smoldering body and stared down at it. "Now get the hell up."

"W-What for?" Marris stuttered in terror.

"We're going to bury her. It's the least we can do."

20

TAKEN AWAY

1989

THE MOMENT HER POINT of view shifted, and she was suddenly looking at a cluster of tree branches, she knew what was happening. Sophia didn't want it to happen, but there was nothing she could do. She tried with all her might to break free from the moment, to remove her consciousness from that place, but it was to no avail. There was nothing to do but be an observer as the murderer trounced their way through the trees. It took several minutes that never seemed to end for the mysterious person to emerge onto something she could identify. As she observed through the killer's eyes, she noticed pavement underfoot and a unique crack that looked familiar.

The mysterious person's gaze lifted to a house in front of them, and Sophia's heart stopped. She screamed, at least she tried to, but nothing came out. After all, she was just a witness. There was nothing tangible she could do as the monster hiding in the skin of a human moved across the yard to the all too familiar side of the house. She tried to convince herself that she was mistaken, that it was a different residence from the one she knew it was. Denying it became impossible when the killer's body phased through the outside wall and exited into the very bedroom she had slept in only a few days prior.

Angie looked so cute snuggled under her covers. So peaceful and unaware of the horrible thing that lurked over her. The last thing Sophia wanted to do was watch what was going to happen next. So, instead of accepting her passive role, she tried to fight with everything she had. Every ounce of her essence, she placed into making something tangible happen. She tried to forcefully stop the murderer from walking across the room to her friend's bed. Then she put forth all her energy to stop the claws from growing out of the killer's fingers. When none of that worked, desperation set in. She looked at Angie through the eyes of the person who was going to murder her, and she screamed.

Sophia was so hellbent on doing something that a shriek actually came from her and filled the room. "Stay away from her!"

That was enough to stop the killer's hands during their movement. Was the murderer hesitating? Perhaps they were simply bewildered by the scream that had come from nowhere. Either way, they had come to a halt, and that was enough time for Angie to begin stirring in her bed.

Driven by her success, Sophia cried out, with it audibly being heard, "They're going to kill you!"

Seconds later, Angie opened her eyes, and the look of confusion quickly turned to one of panic. Sophia tried her best to help her friend at that moment. She desperately tried to wrestle control of the stranger's right arm as they brought it back. It hung there, not moving for several seconds, giving her hope. Then, Angie opened her mouth to cry out for help, and the murderer's limb flew forth with inhuman speed. A wet, gurgling noise that she was all too familiar with joined the sight of blood seeping out from her friend's neck. It was a dribble at first, but then quickly the crimson poured from the open wound. She stared at the shocked expression on Angie's face as she struggled to breathe, her hands wildly pressing against the open wound in an inadequate attempt to stop the bleeding.

As if things could not get any worse, the murderer moved once more, its claws digging into Angie. Skin easily tore open, allowing more crimson to spew forth, leaking all over the bed. Sophia continued her efforts to get the deadly hands to cease, but they tore into her friend without pause. Chunks of flesh began to get tugged loose from the body, and she could see the light quickly fading from her lover's eyes. She felt completely helpless once more, and at that moment she screamed. She screamed with everything she had, and that's when she woke up in her own bed.

The fresh images of the person she loved most being torn apart flashed through her mind as she sat up. Overwhelmed by the magnitude of it all, she did the only thing that her brain allowed her to do. She cried.

Sophia cried when Sister Tamera came to check on her.

She cried throughout the whole search for Angie's body.

She cried when they finally found her girlfriend's torn and empty skin.

Ironically, the only time she didn't weep was at the funeral of her beloved. Instead, she stared off into space thinking about the person that had done this to her. In bed that night, she stared up at the ceiling, silently hoping that the murderer would come for her next.

21

SOMETHING IS OFF

"THAT WASN'T RIGHT."

"What the hell are you complaining about now? You wanted to eat too, so why are you whining?"

"I'm not whining about that. The voice. The voice that interrupted us. That shouldn't have happened. Who was that?"

"Does it matter? We got to eat."

"Of course it matters! They spoke through us. I don't know how, but they did. If they did it once, they can do it again."

"Let them speak. They weren't strong enough to stop us. What good is a voice if it doesn't accomplish anything?"

"It starts as just a voice, but what if they can feed as well? If they can grow their strength, then they might very well pose a threat before too long."

"Don't be ridiculous. No one can stop us. Can't you tell? This energy. The power from that last meal is incredible! Even if that voice could become more, there's no way they could match our might."

"A threat is a threat, no matter how minor it is. It would be foolish for us to disregard it. After all, it hasn't been long since our hibernation. We're still vulnerable, whether you think so or not."

"If you truly believe that someone can hurt us, there is only one way to protect ourselves."

"I...I know, and...you're right."

"What? Are you serious? We get to feast?"

"Yes. Unfortunately, yes. We will still have to be strategic about it, but we need to feed. That voice...it was trying to warn that girl. She was important to them, and we killed her. No doubt the owner of that voice will be coming for vengeance. We must be prepared, otherwise, all we've done will be in vain."

22

THROUGH THE WINDOW

1989

SHE HEARD SISTER TAMERA'S footsteps but didn't bother to look. Even when she felt her presence in the doorway of her bedroom, she refused to turn. Sophia simply stared out the window that had nothing to offer her but a dismal view of a collection of bare trees, all their leaves having fallen off weeks prior. She didn't want to talk, but clearly, her guardian wanted to. There was nothing to talk about. All she longed for was to wallow in sorrow. Anything that took away from that was nothing more than a nuisance.

"I'm getting ready to make dinner. I was thinking of whipping up some pork chops. They're still one of your favorites, right?"

Sophia saw the question for what it was, a sad attempt to get her to talk. She didn't take the bait. Instead, she wordlessly shook her head as a response.

Tamera let out a long sigh. "I haven't seen you eat yet this week." When she was met by silence, she took a step into the room. "You need to eat something. You're going to starve yourself to death doing this."

"Good."

"Don't say that," Tamera gasped. Despite her ward clearly not wanting her in there, she moved over and had a seat on the bed. "You giving up on living won't help anything."

Sophia scoffed. "Of course it would. Every single person I care for dies, and everyone else despises me. It doesn't matter where I go, I can feel the hateful stares. I still look like a little kid, and I don't feel right in my body. The world hates me, and I hate it. So why shouldn't I do it, huh? Because your religion says I shouldn't?"

"No," Tamera answered softly, "because I would miss you so much."

"What?" Sophia said with shock. She wasn't expecting to be met with such kindness, and it was enough to finally turn her focus from the window.

Tamera couldn't help but chuckle lightly. "Why do you sound so surprised? You've been living with me for several years now. Of course, I wouldn't want you to die. I care about you so much." She paused briefly , then tentatively continued, "In fact...I think of you as my daughter. And even though we're not flesh and blood, I hope you think of me as a surrogate mother of sorts."

"I..." Sophia tried to speak, but a lump formed in her throat. She was overwhelmed with emotion to the point where her mind was scattered with incoherent thoughts.

After several moments of her love not being reciprocated, a flash of hurt crossed Tamera's face. "Oh...it's okay if you don't, of course. I understand. I just hope that one day..."

Sophia interrupted by suddenly wrapping her arms around her guardian in a passionate hug. "I do feel the same way," she whispered as a few tears trickled out of her eyes. "I just...I didn't think anyone else cared about me that much."

Tamera gently rubbed Sophia's back for several seconds, then softly asked, "You mean as much as Angie did?"

Sophia pulled back from the hug so she could look her guardian in the eyes. There was something implied in the question. It made it seem that Tamera knew about her and Angie. Based on that assumption, she expected to be met with a look of disgust, but that wasn't the case. Instead, the eyes staring at her were filled with empathy and understanding.

"Did...did you know?" she meekly asked. She didn't elaborate on what she meant as shame flushed her cheeks.

"I had my suspicions but didn't know for sure." Her lips curled into a soft smile as she added, "Of course, it was none of my business. You were so happy, and that's all that mattered."

"You're...not mad at me?"

"No, of course I'm not," Tamera responded with sincerity. "Love is love. It doesn't matter what shape, size, or form it comes in. I truly believe that."

Sophia sat there in stunned silence. The kindness and understanding folded through her. Joy and other emotions she never thought she would feel again after Angie's murder were bubbling to the surface. She wanted to shower Tamera with so much affection, but no words came to mind. No matter how hard she tried, she couldn't think of something substantive to say.

Instead, when she finally opened her mouth, all that came out was, "Thank you."

In response, Tamera placed a hand on her left shoulder and smiled, "Of course."

With that, her guardian stood up and moved over to the doorway, but paused at the threshold. She turned back to Sophia and asked, "I'm going to get started on dinner. Will you be eating?"

Still awash with positivity, all Sophia could muster was a nod. That was all that was needed and her adoptive mother headed off to the kitchen. Though she was once again sitting by herself, there was a completely different feeling to it. Now there was hope. It seemed like she had a legitimate chance to be happy. Maybe not right away, but eventually. After she processed Angie's death and her grief diminished, perhaps she could move on. Tamera accepted her for who she was, and that was more important than anything else. Through the good and bad times, her adoptive mother would be there for her.

Suddenly, the vision of the gnarled hands belonging to the murderous stranger flashed through her mind. Just like that, all her optimism evaporated into nothing. There was no hope of happiness. Not while that freak had the ability to phase into people's houses and kill at will. She had no doubt that the murderer would eventually come for her or Tamera. As long as that thing remained alive, Sophia could not live a happy life. She had to put a stop to them. Whoever they were, their killing spree had to come to an end, and she was going to do it or die trying.

Some of this newfound resolve was for her own well-being, but most of it was for Tamera. She didn't deserve to die like Angie and Travers did. No one did. So, as quietly as possible, she got up from her bed and carefully opened the window. As she snuck out of the comfort of her home, she mentally readied herself for what lay ahead. Without much thought, she began walking in the direction of the woods. She had a notion that if she simply made it there, something beyond herself would guide her directly to the killer.

23

IT'S NOT A TUMOR

1974

ROY FIDGETED ON THE exam chair as he impatiently waited for the doctor, the paper crinkling each time he moved about. Suddenly, the door creaked open, and he came to an abrupt halt. He anxiously watched as the older gentleman waddled into the room, adorned in his medical coat. Wordlessly, the doctor sat down in the swivel chair positioned a few feet in front of him and then silently opened a file, examining the contents within it. After roughly half a minute without anything happening, Roy became antsy, so much so that he had to say something.

He tried his best to hide his anxiety by taking on a tone of annoyance as he grumbled, "So what in the hell is so important that you had to drag me in here instead of just telling me over the phone?" Roy was met by silence, which legitimately irritated him, "Dr. Barton? Paul, are you listening to me?"

Barton finally looked up from the file with a grave expression. "Well, truth be told, I could have told you over the phone, but I thought it would be better to do so in person."

Roy's heart sank into his stomach. "Is it that bad, Doc?"

"I wouldn't necessarily say it's bad. It's just...well...let's just say it's downright weird. I doubt you would believe me without some proof." Barton pulled an X-ray image from the folder, then stood up and moved over to stand right beside Roy. "After examining your x-rays I happened to notice a growth around your abdominal and pelvic region. You see it right there?"

"Yeah."

"That's what's causing all your discomfort. It's reached a large enough size that it's pressing up on all your organs and other body parts in that area," Barton explained with a small hint of uneasiness in his voice.

"Ummm...okay, but what is it?"

There was a long and drawn-out pause before the doctor answered, "I honestly don't know for sure."

"You don't know!" Roy exclaimed, totally incensed. "Is it a tumor? A turd that somehow snuck out? Do you have a damn guess even?"

"I have a guess," Barton snapped.

"Then what is it?"

All the anger from Barton's reply fizzled out, only to be replaced with hesitancy. "Well, I can't be sure but...but I think it might be a fetus."

"I don't...that doesn't make any sense. I'm a man!" Roy shouted while pounding his fist on his knee. "I think I might need to get me a new doctor."

"I know it seems strange..."

"You fucking think? I should have known you were just a quack trying to take my money. I mean, how the hell did you come up with something so stupid?" he snapped.

Barton held up a hand and calmly replied, "If you just let me walk you through my reasoning, I think you'll understand where I'm coming from, okay?" He took the silence that followed as an answer and continued, "Good. Now, if we retake a look at that growth, you can see that it's a peculiar shape. I ruled out this being a tumor based on this. Tumors don't have to be circular or oval, but they certainly wouldn't take on this form. So, that left me in a conundrum that had me staring at this X-ray for hours until I noticed this little bit right here."

Roy stared at the area the doctor was pointing at, but due to the mysterious growth being so faint in the scan, he couldn't make anything out. "What am I supposed to be seeing?"

"In truth, not much," Barton replied as he taped the image with his finger, "but based on my assumptions, this part that is slightly breaking off from the rest of the growth is the beginnings of an arm."

"How do you know it's an arm for sure?"

"I don't, but it's the only explanation that makes sense."

"No, it's not!" Roy began shouting again. "Men don't get pregnant. They fucking can't! Everybody knows that. It's Biology 101 and you don't know that? Shit, you're a terrible doctor."

Barton's patience wore thin from the insult, and he bluntly replied, "If it's a tumor, then you're dead." That was enough to cut the yelling off and give him a chance to explain some more. "A tumor about the size of a tangerine is basically a death sentence. The only alternative, the sole other option that makes sense besides a tumor, is a fetus."

"But...how?"

The doctor shrugged in complete bewilderment. "I have absolutely no fucking idea. This defies all known logic in the field of medicine. Hell, this violates biology itself. For the life of me, I can't think of anything that would explain this."

"So...what do we do then?" Roy asked, anxiety leaking from his voice.

Barton let out a deep sigh as he delivered some unpleasant news. "The only thing we can do is wait."

"Wait? I've got a fucking baby growing inside of me and you're telling me to wait!"

"We don't know that for sure," Barton countered. "We'll give it another two weeks, then have you back for more x-rays. If it is truly a fetus, then it will have grown and developed a bit more. I'll be able to see that. Plus, it gives me time."

"Time to do what?"

"Time to think through what the hell we're going to do here," Barton shook his head as he placed the scan back into the folder. "I've never heard of a man getting an abortion. Hell, I don't even know how it'd be done, but that might end up being our only option." He tucked the folder under his arm and moved to the door. As he opened it, he added, "You might want to get your affairs in order."

Then the doctor left, leaving Roy to sit there in stunned silence with the thing that was growing inside of him.

24

WOODED ENCOUNTER

1989

THE TREES ALL LOOKED the same to her. Each one was bare and seemed to be near death. There were seemingly no identifiable features to differentiate one from another. This would likely cause someone less in tune with the world around them to panic, but Sophia was locked in. Something beyond her own abilities was guiding her along, though she couldn't explain exactly what it was. Simply put, it was a feeling, a sensation that tugged her in the correct direction to go. Though she was in a spot of the woods with no visible exit, she believed there was no need to worry.

A gentle gust of autumn wind blew through her hair, and she allowed herself a moment of inaction. She stood perfectly still as she closed her eyes and took a long breath. The exhale from her lips soothed her spirit, which in turn created the drive to push on. She continued while the sun dipped down in the sky behind her. After a few more minutes spent walking, dusk had set in, and visibility was becoming slim. The intangible guide was still directing her along, but Sophia's own doubts began to set in. Her confidence went with the sun, so by the time the moon had shown itself, she had become somewhat weary.

The mission, the very thing she had come to the woods to accomplish, became an afterthought in light of the anxious ideas that began to cloud her head. Light noises that had not bothered her a short time before now made her antsy. This in turn led to her quickening her pace to that of a fast walk. In this state of weakness, she allowed her emotions and not the invisible force to guide her. Instead of progressing with confidence and purpose, she was wandering about aimlessly through the sickened trees. As the last bits of sunlight dipped out of view, she began to scrape herself against the branches. This only worked to heighten the anxiety already plaguing her mind.

Suddenly, a sound cut through the night like a razor-sharp knife through flesh. A voice hissed at a volume just above a whisper. *"We knew you would come."*

Immediately terror wrestled control of her body from her rational-thinking brain and sent it sprinting off into the woods. Along with the rapid gasps of air she was taking in and the snapping of twigs underneath her feet, Sophia could hear gusts of wind whipping about behind her. An enormous and blood-curdling cackle filled the air, which shot a pure ball of dread directly into her gut. She tried to accelerate more but found that her legs would not oblige. Her body had reached its top speed, and that was definitely not good, as she could sense the horrific thing closing in.

She dared not glance behind her. Not because she might risk losing her balance, but because the thought of what she might see was too much for her to withstand. Sophia blew past trees, ignoring the branches as they scratched at her skin. She was thankful that it hadn't rained recently, so the ground was solid, and she could easily maneuver over it. Another cackle broke her focus from directly in front of her, and she couldn't help but take the quickest peek using the periphery of her vision. All she was able to make out was the shadow of something moving over the ground, while the figure that was making it wasn't touching dirt. Whatever the thing chasing her was, it was flying.

Pure terror gripped her insides as she continued onward. Despite things seeming hopeless, she hadn't been caught yet. Perhaps there was a chance that she would be able to escape the monstrosity. This hope was diminished when a tree branch suddenly moved itself into the path directly in front of her. Sophia was only just able to dodge the limb, but seconds later another positioned itself to obstruct her. She found herself maneuvering her way around branches that were moving of their own accord. This thing had nature on its side.

After a few minutes of desperately dodging, the wooden limbs finally began to grab at her. She managed to rip herself free from the first few attempts, but one managed to wrap itself around her leg. Sophia went to pull it off her, but another branch restricted her right arm. Quickly, dozens of wooden limbs wrapped themselves around her, trapping her. She kicked and screamed, but it was no use; there was no fighting it. The thing that had been chasing her flew overhead, passing her before circling back around and slowly descending to the ground. Thanks to the lack of illumination, she could only make out the shape of a woman as their feet touched down.

"Finally, I have you," the mysterious woman said with a surprisingly gentle voice.

Then, Sophia lost consciousness.

25

His Last Night

1974

THE PAIN WAS ABSOLUTELY unbearable. It was so debilitating that all he could do was lie there and stare at the ceiling of his bedroom. He had been like that all day, unable to move for fear of making things worse, so he stayed completely still. The only thing Roy was able to accomplish was to groan in agony, with a constant sound emitting from his cracked, chapped lips. All the moaning had dried out his throat, and even that was adding to the pain that seemed to wrack every inch of his body. There was no fighting this thing, whatever it was. In his head, he silently repeated to himself that this thing was going to kill him.

He still couldn't believe the doctor had simply told him to wait. Only five days had passed since that completely pointless appointment, and he had been reduced to a glorified vegetable. Roy couldn't work the day after receiving the news. He had been forced to leave mid-shift due to the agony pulsating through his abdominal region. Then, the following day, he found himself barely able to move around his house. That led to him being mostly bedridden, though he was still able to move about on occasion. But not today. There was too much pain. Instead of getting up to go to the bathroom, he had just soiled himself. Feces and piss stained his clothes as well as the bed, but he didn't care. That didn't matter to him while he was suffering this much.

Yesterday, he had reached out to Dr. Barton, desperate that the medical professional had something, but he didn't. Instead, he told Roy the same thing he had before. He could hear it in Barton's voice; the man didn't know what to do. That meant it was all over. His fate was officially sealed. There was nothing else left to try but to lie there and hope for a miracle. Amidst the agony and the putrid stench filling the room, he attempted something he hadn't done in years; he prayed. He gave it everything he had, but of course, nothing responded to him. There would be no salvation for him as he was beyond saving.

As if to emphasize his doom, a sudden spasm of agony revved up around his pelvic region. He screamed out for mercy while waiting for the wave of pain to subside, but it did not. That's when he realized that the growth was moving about inside of him. It seemed to be kicking at his organs in an attempt to accomplish something. Through all the hurt, it clicked for him; it was trying to escape. After all, according to Dr. Barton, it was a fetus, and apparently the time had come for it to be born. He knew this thing was going to try to force its way out of him, but there was no discernible opening for it to do so.

Roy said a final prayer that his death would be swift and come well before the crime against nature ripped through him. Immediately, the agony that had already been debilitating doubled in intensity as his wails grew louder. His screams grew so loud that they ceased to come from his throat, like a shut-off had been activated inside his body. The kicking continued as the growth began to wriggle about, bumping into and further smashing his organs. He had been right that it was going to be the death of him; it just came sooner than he expected.

The unnatural thing forced itself downward through his abdominal region until Roy felt it become stuck against something. He begged for it all to end, but the growth started to press against the obstruction. His body part did not last long, and when the abomination broke through, an indescribable wave of agony flooded over him. It wasted no time and continued its unholy push through him. The horrific ordeal took dozens of minutes until it reached his perineum, and by that point he was barely holding on. Roy was alive just long enough to endure another barrage of agony as an infant body tore the first hole that ripped open his skin. As crimson gushed out over the bed, he took his final breath.

26

UNWANTED ANSWERS

1989

IT WAS A TEARING noise combined with grunting that gradually pulled her towards consciousness. As she began to stir, Sophia felt her back pressed up against something hard. Slowly, she opened her eyes and was greeted by an area with not much in terms of illumination. There was a lone, dimly lit fire in the center of the space that cast shadows upon the smooth walls and added an eeriness to things. She turned to her right and saw a natural stone floor. It took her glancing upward at the ceiling to realize she was in a cave. This confused her, as she'd never heard of any caves existing in Shallowroot.

Her befuddlement was short-lived as another tearing noise brought her attention to the feral woman only a few feet to her left. The supernatural hag snarled as she bit at something strongly clutched in her hands. Sophia focused on the object, only to immediately regret doing so. It was an arm with some flesh still clinging to the bone, and the monstrous woman was eagerly trying to tear chunks of meat away. Only a few more seconds passed before she spotted the skeletal human hand still attached to the limb. There was no stopping her reaction as her body gagged at the sight of such a horrific scene. In response, the feral hag whirled about in her direction, then flashed a smile while continuing to chew on the meat in her mouth.

"You're awake."

"Fuck me," Sophia whispered.

She gazed at the burnt face that stared at her, taking in the horror of it. Patches of burnt skin covered the scalp, interrupted by random clumps of hair. Malicious intent was plain to see in the hag's eyes, while tattered and burned clothes barely clung to her, not leaving much to the imagination. The private parts of the feral thing were also covered in burns and scars. Sophia also noticed that there was an indent on the right breast, where a nipple had been forcibly removed.

The woman was truly a monstrous sight to behold, and Sophia couldn't help but mutter, "I'm going to die here."

"What? No. Why would you think that?" the hag responded as the ill intent left her eyes.

Sophia was taken aback by the voice that sounded normal and that in no way fit the vision of what was before her. Even more so, she was shocked that the animalistic murderer had responded to her in a caring manner. It took several moments in the silence for her to realize she had been given a golden opportunity. The freak didn't want to kill her just yet. She could talk to it and hopefully get some answers. At the very least, there was a possibility that she could buy herself some time.

"I woke up to you ripping apart a human arm," Sophia bluntly answered. "You've been killing for years. Why shouldn't I be afraid?"

"Because I don't want to kill," the scarred lady replied, still using a normal voice.

Sophia scoffed in a kneejerk response and immediately regretted it. The little outburst could send the person into a rage, and then she would end up being the one getting snacked on. Quickly, she tried to pivot the focus off her raw reaction by asking, "If you don't want to kill, then why do it?"

"I have to."

"You have to?" Sophia said incredulously. "What would make you need to kill someone?"

"We are weak."

The sudden return of the inhuman voice caused Sophia to jump a bit as a rush of adrenaline kicked in. She pressed her back firmly against the wall as she asked, "W-What was that? Why did you talk like that?"

"That's...that's my other half," the normal voice answered. "There are two of us inside here. We each occupy this body. It used to be just me, but now I must coexist."

"Is it...is it human?" Sophia asked with morbid curiosity.

The hag shook her scarred head. "No. I don't know what it is exactly, but it's not human. Some would probably call it a demon, or a monster. I'm not certain if it is either of those. All I know is that it is a part of me now."

That response left a natural opening for Sophia to ask the most important question that had been on her mind for some time. "And who are you?"

"I used to be Teresa Stillwater, but that was a long time ago. I don't think I can still call myself that, not after everything that's happened," the killer said as she fully sat down, her muscles relaxing.

Sophia picked up on the body language, and that gave her the confidence to loosen up a bit, but she did not relax a significant amount just in case an opportunity to escape presented itself to her. "You were burned. The factory workers, they burned you. Why did they do it?"

A hardened scowl appeared on the hag's face as she replied, "Bigotry was why some of them did it, others because of fear, and a few just got swept up in the mob. But most wanted to take advantage of me and then cut me down. Either way, a man, a real piece of shit, Roy Tyler, started the whole thing. He convinced a dozen or so that I was dangerous. Got them all riled up with these ridiculous lies and then led them right to my door. By then, they were no better than a pack of wild dogs." She paused to pick up a random bone sitting on the ground and flick it toward the back of the cave. "I would have preferred a pack of dogs."

Sophia was hesitant to ask, but her curiosity overrode her better judgment. "They did more than burn you, didn't they?"

An intensity flashed in Teresa's eyes as she began, "First they broke into my home, dragged me out of it, and beat me to the point where I could barely stand. I remember being so scared to die." She let out a harsh chuckle. "All that punishment and I didn't bleed out. A shame. A damn shame."

"So, they beat you and then burned you?"

Teresa shook her head. "No, they did worse after they dragged me into the woods. Up to that point, out where the civilized world could see them, they were still people. But the second the trees hid them, they became animals. They dragged me to the first open area, and then Roy made them hold me down..." She trailed off, staring down at her feet until she lifted her gaze to meet Sophia's and she angrily snapped, "He had his way with me! Then that fucker let the others take their turns. They raped me! In front of all their friends, those animals took turns raping me!"

"Holy shit," Sophia whispered.

She had come there with nothing but hate in her heart and vengeance on her mind, and yet, she was feeling an inkling of sympathy for the woman who had caused so much suffering in her life. What Teresa had been put through; she couldn't even begin to imagine it. The whole thing was disgusting beyond words, and part of her felt the need to comfort the broken woman.

Sophia softly whispered, "I'm so sorry."

"Sorry does nothing!"

Just as soon as it had arrived, the inhuman voice left to be replaced with Teresa's calmer tone saying, "Thank you. It doesn't change anything but thank you."

That terrifying outburst erased all traces of empathy that had been building inside of Sophia. She needed that to remind her that she was dealing with a killer who ate their victims. Terrible crimes may have been committed against Teresa, but she had also orchestrated many of her own. The thing sitting before her was no longer a victim or even a person for that matter. The hag was a vicious beast, nothing more than an unhinged lunatic who needed to be stopped at all costs. A story wouldn't change that, and with her resolve back in place, Sophia would make sure she ended the bitch the first moment she could.

"It lasted hours," Teresa continued, with anger still leaking from her voice. "They brought a priest with them."

"A priest?" Sophia repeated. She pondered who that could have been then blurted out, "Father Marris!" The memory of the fire came rushing back to her, and she remembered the nuns talking about how he had perished in the flames.

Teresa nodded. "Roy had convinced him that I was possessed. That a servant of the devil had taken hold of my body. They brought along Father Marris for divine protection. He didn't do much of that while they were raping me!" she snapped. "I called out to him. Begged him to save me, show me mercy. Help in any way...but he didn't. He just stood there and watched with that stupid, fake horrified expression smeared across his fucking face!" Teresa sneered. "That fucker liked what he was watching, I could tell. His eyes gave him away."

"That dirty bastard was hard! He was getting off on it."

"You started the fire, the one that burned down the orphanage," Sophia realized. "That was all so you could kill Father Marris? Someone else could have died. I almost did!"

"But you didn't."

"We weren't trying to hurt anyone else. Definitely not you. The only reason we started the fire was so no one knew about us," Teresa chimed in with her human voice.

"Stop saying 'we'," Sophia ordered. "There is no 'we'. There's just you. No one else is here."

Teresa frowned as a hint of anger flared up in her pupils, "I already told you I share this body with something inhuman. After they took their turns, the disgusting pigs, they led me further into the woods where they built a pyre and tied me to it. Again, I begged for mercy, and again, they gave me none." She locked eyes with Sophia as she asked, "Have you ever been burnt? And not just the tip of your finger, or some small part of your skin. I mean burnt to the point where you can smell your own flesh cooking."

"I..."

"Of course not. It's the worst pain you could imagine. In all that agony, I called out, not to heaven, but to hell. They thought I was in with the devil, so I reached out to him, and he respond-ed. This thing that now lives with me is what I was given. It kept me alive, though it did nothing to stop the flames from burning my body. That's okay though. I live. That is what matters."

Sophia once again pressed her back against the cave wall as Teresa's intensity scared her a bit. That fear didn't overpower her curiosity, however, and she inquired, "So, when did you take your revenge?"

"I had to wait. After everything, my body was broken, inside and out. It needed to heal, but when that was all done, I was reborn. I became the very thing they had tried to kill me for being. And with that power, I gave them all the most incredible curse I could imagine."

"What?" Sophia asked, somewhat fearful of the answer.

Teresa's lips curled in an evil smirk. "They impregnated me against my will, so I did the same to them. Of course, since men's bodies can't give birth, their offspring forcefully came into the world. I wish I could have been there to witness it unfold, but the curse itself left us too weak. We needed to sleep. And we did for nearly half a decade."

"W-What?" Sophia stuttered as a horrible realization was starting to come together in her mind. "You had a kid?"

Teresa's smirk turned into a much gentler smile. "Well, that's interesting. You didn't know? Hmmm, I thought you would have at least suspected something with the visions. Haven't you ever noticed that you age slower than everyone else? That...and the birthmark, of course. It's a symbol, a sign of what you are. That alone should have told you. I suppose that's all right. That means I get to tell you the truth. I had you. I'm your mother."

Overwhelmed by the information that part of her knew was true, she tried to deny it. "No. No, no, no! You killed everyone I've ever loved! You can't be my mother!"

A laugh escaped from the witch's maw. "That you loved? You mean the old man? He was nothing, a nobody who buried us alive. He had to pay for his sins, plain and simple. Surely you can't be mad about that."

"You murdered Angie!" Sophia screamed as her emotions got the better of her. Tears began to form in the corner of her eyes.

"Angie? A friend of yours?" Teresa raised what was left of her right eyebrow as she studied Sophia with intrigue. "Oh wait! The one you spoke through us for. She was the one you tried to wrestle control from us for. Interesting...why so much effort for a friend?"

"She wasn't just a friend!" Sophia shouted. "She was so much more than that."

"Oh," Teresa reacted with a look of disgust.

"Ha! Looks like our daughter has a thing for girls."

"That's okay," Teresa stated as she returned to her normal voice. "It doesn't matter anymore. Now that you're here, we can be together."

Sophia's anger boiled over, and she spat at the witch, "Fuck you!"

"You have to stay, please! I'm your mother."

"No, you're not! You abandoned me, then killed everyone who ever looked after me. You're a fucking monster. I'd rather die than stay with you."

Teresa shook her head. "You don't mean that. You don't." She moved to where she was leaning toward Sophia while sitting on her knees. "You're a witch, just like me. That's why you look so young, because of your power. It means you age slower than everyone else. It also means you'll never fit in. They'll all hate you. You'll never be loved by them. But I love you. I'll take care of you."

Sophia grimaced with displeasure at the idea of having to be around such an awful person, and that notion made her sick to her stomach. "Are you going to kill me or what?" she asked. When no response came, she locked eyes with the witch. "Because if you don't kill me, I'm going to kill you."

"Okay, it's time to stop playing around and accept..."

"Someone is here!"

"What? It must be a child who got lost in the woods, or a hunter who wandered too far," Teresa insisted.

"No, it's an assassin brought here by our bastard. She means to kill us!"

With near-inhuman speed, Teresa grabbed Sophia and lifted her off the ground by her neck. The witch held her there for several seconds and then threw her down. As her back connected with the ground, the air was knocked from her lungs, and she struggled to breathe.

"We will deal with your friend first, and then it will be your turn, you back-stabbing bitch."

27

———

A DESPERATE SEARCH

1989

IT TOOK ROUGHLY A dozen knocks, but finally, the door swung open to reveal the irritated face of the woman of the house. When she realized Tamera was the one knocking, her features softened, and she put on a faux smile.

"Sister, I wasn't expecting you. What can I do for you?"

Tamera ignored the fakery as she was on a mission. "I was wondering if you had seen Sophia by chance. She left before dinner last night, and she hasn't come back home."

The homeowner's fake smile turned to a small frown as she shook her head. "Umm, no. I haven't seen anything."

Something was off in the woman's tone, so Tamera pressed the matter. "Are you sure? You didn't see her walking around last night or maybe heard something this morning?"

"Nope, can't say that I did," the homeowner replied, though her pleasant tone was slipping and some of her annoyance was leaking through.

It was easy to pick up on what was happening; she was quickly overstaying her welcome. However, part of Tamera wasn't going to put up with it. She had been dealing with the disrespectful attitude from every person she interacted with all morning, and she was fed up. Normally, she would have held her tongue and moved on, but she had reached a breaking point. She was looking for her adoptive daughter, someone she loved, and everyone treated her like a leper. It was clear that if she hadn't been a nun, the community would have completely ostracized her just because she was caring for Sophia, and that was unacceptable.

"You would have slammed the door in my face if I wasn't a nun," Tamera stated, not as a question but as a fact.

The homeowner scoffed at the statement, "I don't know where that came from, but I wo-"

"You know that lying is a sin." Tamera cut off the woman before she could say anything else. "Doing so to a disciple of God, well...that's probably even worse."

A scowl appeared on the homeowner's face. "You know what, fine. You're right. If I wasn't afraid of facing the wrath of God, I would have slammed the door in your face. You want to know why?" She leaned forward and whispered, "Because you've got that freak living under your roof."

"She's not a freak. She is a child, just like all the others in this town."

"Except she isn't," the homeowner shot back. "There's something wrong with her. I don't know what it is, but I can see it, and so can everyone else. Since she was brought into this world, terrible things have been happening to people in this town. It doesn't take a genius to connect the dots."

Tamera blinked several times in disbelief at what was being said. "You're not serious, are you? You're blaming a child for what's been going wrong in Shallowroot? How old was she when the murders started, hmm? Eight, nine, maybe ten? Do you honestly believe a ten-year-old was going around killing people?"

"I never said she killed anyone," the homeowner shot back. "But there's an evil around that girl. It may not be her, but it follows her. Bad things happen when she's involved, and everyone can see that except for you. She's cursed, and everyone she comes into contact with suffers because of it." She paused to let it sink in, then added, "For your sake, I hope she stays gone."

Before Tamera could respond, the door was slammed in her face, leaving her standing there, fuming. The people of the town had let superstition and fear run their lives for far too long, and now she was seeing the damage it could do firsthand. They were blaming a child for their misfortune instead of accepting things for what they were and moving on. She wanted to break down the door and scream some common sense into the homeowner, but that wouldn't solve anything. Sophia was still out there somewhere, and she had to find her. That was the only thing that mattered.

She walked down the driveway while glancing at the surrounding houses. Thanks to hours of work, she had knocked on every door in the neighborhood, and it had gotten her nowhere. No one was going to help her; she was on her own. Tamera took a deep breath and tried to think like Sophia. Where would she have gone? What could have possibly been going on inside her head the night prior? She mulled it over for a few moments before concluding that Angie was the likely answer. That also meant that the murderer must have been on her adopted child's mind. But where would that train of thought have taken her?

As she started to aimlessly move down the street, she pondered that question. Tamera reviewed all the conversations she had with Sophia over the past couple of months, trying to find some pertinent detail. All she could remember was the grief her adopted daughter felt over losing her friend—no—her love. That kind of loss would cause a lot of intense emotions, rage probably being one of the strongest. Perhaps...perhaps she had snuck out with vengeance on her mind. That was certainly an alarming thought, but that still didn't tell her where Sophia could have gone.

She decided to pivot her thinking to ask where a killer was most likely to hide in Shallowroot. Since Sophia more than likely went after Angie's murderer, then she probably ventured to the perfect hiding place for a criminal. There weren't many buildings in the town besides houses, so not many options for such a place became apparent. She racked her brain, trying to solve her conundrum. As Tamera walked, she brought her gaze to the large patch of trees that designated the end of the neighborhood, and that's when the answer came to her. The woods. Sophia had gone into the woods, so that's where she would go too.

28

SUPERSTITIOUS WARNINGS

1974

SISTER ANNA GLANCED UP from her papers as the door opened. "Ah, Sister Tamera, please come in. Oh, do shut the door behind you."

The new member of the congregation did as she was told, then crossed over and had a seat in one of the two worn chairs placed before the senior nun's desk.

"Out of curiosity, Sister, what is this meeting about?" Tamera asked with nervousness in her voice.

Anna tried to dismiss her worries with a chuckle. "You're not in any trouble if that's what you're wondering. No, I just wanted to see how you were doing. We have a large responsibility on our hands to shape and mold the youth of this town. If we don't perform each day to the best of our abilities, there's a very good chance these poor children could be without a home."

"Of course, Sister," Tamera responded with a subservient nod.

There was a sizable stretch of silence as Sister Anna decided how best to handle the conversation until she inquired, "How are things with the children? It's not too much, is it?"

"No, not at all. It can be...tiring...but rewarding at the same time. I enjoy helping where there is a need," Tamera answered. She glanced over at the small rays of light shining through the lone window in the room then asked, "What happened, Sister? Why was there such a sudden influx of children? Surely fifteen in one week is not the norm, right? Where did they all come from?"

Anna ignored the questions. "The others tell me you have been very diligent and caring with the children. You should be proud." She took a deep breath then added, "Though...it seems you've been particularly focused on one child."

Tamera looked at her superior, puzzled. "Is that a problem?"

"Well, no. Not normally."

"Not normally? Is there something I should know?"

Anna placed both hands flat on the desk as she responded, "It's just that...Sophia is a bit...different from the other children. For one, she's older, and hence probably doesn't require as much attention."

"But she's a toddler. Most of the other children are infants. I'd argue she requires more supervision since she can move about on her own."

"Well, we have other Sisters to help out with that, so you can focus more of your attention to helping out with the newborns," Anna replied, gently hinting that she was giving an order.

"Why? Why do I need to change what I am doing if others agree that I'm doing a good job?" Tamera demanded to know.

Anna narrowed her gaze. "Is it common for you to question your superiors like this?"

"It is if they tell me conflicting things," Tamera bluntly answered.

Dumbfounded by the sudden gall of the woman sitting before her, Anna sat silent for a moment. She shook her head. "Very well, I'll be straightforward with you since that's clearly what you are after. Sophia is not a regular child. You've only been here for a few months, so you don't realize it yet, but she is not like any child you have ever met."

Tamera scoffed, "Are you telling me to avoid her simply because she is different? That's ridiculous!"

Anna shook her head. "I don't think you understood me. She is different, true, but more so than you are probably thinking. You see...it's..." she was struggling to find a way to explain things before finally asking, "Do you know how long she's been with us?" Tamera shook her head. "Almost five years. That child that you said was a toddler just a moment ago is actually the age of someone that should be in preschool or kindergarten right now."

"Okay, so she has some type of disability. There are disorders where someone looks younger than they actually are. That's no reason to treat them differently."

A sigh of annoyance escaped Anna's lips. She tried to remain calm as she explained, "It's not a disorder. Sophia is literally aging slower than the rest of us. There is a supernatural presence around her, and it has a sinister intent. I am telling you this now for your own safety."

Tamera stood up and exclaimed, "This is ridiculous! You are alienating a child because of what? A notion? A superstitious feeling? You can't prove that she's aging slower than everyone else. It's just a hunch."

"It's not just a hunch. I have seen it with my own eyes, and it is the truth," Anna insisted.

"Either way, she is a child. An *innocent* child, and I will not treat her differently from anyone else."

"You will," Anna demanded. She didn't want to use her authority, but it seemed like she was left no other choice. "From now on you are under strict orders to tend to the other children first and foremost. Sophia is to be your last priority, is that clear?"

Tamera turned and wordlessly crossed to the door. As she went to open it, she stopped and turned back to her superior. "Treat others as you would want to be treated," she said with anger dripping from her voice. "It's one of the most fundamental lessons of the Bible, and it seems you might have forgotten it somewhere along the way."

As the younger nun stormed out, Anna placed her head in her hands. That was not the way she wanted that to go, but it was for the young woman's own good. Sophia was dangerous. She was certain that too much interaction with the girl would eventually lead to ruin, though a part of her wondered if she was wrong about the whole situation. Either way, she felt horrible about the matter. It seemed like God truly did give his toughest battles to his strongest warriors.

29

AN END TO THE CARNAGE

1989

With a simple wave of the witch's hand, the fire magically went out, and the area was plunged into darkness, except for the sun shining down on the mouth of the cave. Sophia remained on the ground, still struggling to regain her breath. She couldn't do anything but listen to the footsteps of the supposed assassin as they came to the front of the cave. There was a moment when the footfall ceased, perhaps due to some hesitancy.

Then a familiar voice called out, "Sophia? Are you in there?"

Panic gripped at her insides as she realized that Tamera was about to enter the deathtrap. She tried once more to inhale, and this time managed to suck in a lungful of air. Several tentative steps had already been taken by the time she accomplished this, but she could tell that her adoptive mother was still close to the exit of the cave. There was still time to warn her.

"Get out!" she wheezed out with all her might. Sophia wanted to say more, but a series of coughs ripped their way out of her throat instead.

"Where are you?" Tamera asked in alarm as she moved further into the cave. "What are you doing here?"

Suddenly, the fire started back up, the flames shooting up and licking the stone roof. The sudden illumination stunned Tamera long enough for Teresa to emerge from where she had been hiding toward the back of the cave. The witch charged forth as

the confused nun looked at what was racing toward her with
stunned confusion.

"What is happening?" Tamera asked a moment before a burnt
hand thrust forth and grabbed part of her shirt.

Supernatural strength moved through scarred hands, and the
fully grown woman was lifted into the air before being slammed
onto the solid ground below. Before Tamera had time to recover
from the first attack, the witch had grabbed hold of her hair,
close to the scalp, and forcefully pulled her up onto her knees.

"Don't!" Sophia screamed as she tried to sit up. Pain ravaged
her back, but she fought through it to roll onto her stomach and
lift herself onto her elbows. "Don't you fucking hurt her!"

"Why? So you and your assassin can kill us? I don't think so!"

With that, the witch took Tamera's right arm and snapped it
a few inches above the elbow. A scream of agony filled the cave
as bone poked through the skin of the injured nun. Teresa let
go of her prey, and the broken woman tumbled to the floor.
Rage filled Sophia, and that gave her the strength to get to her
feet. That was short-lived as the witch immediately delivered
a backhand that sent her flying through the air. She connected
with a side wall and her body fell to the earth, landing in a pile
of broken bones.

"Is this your best effort to kill us? It's pathetic!"

"We're not trying to kill you!" Sophia insisted with a groan as
she rolled off the pile of bones. A broken femur with a jagged
point came rolling along as well, stopping only a few inches from
her.

Tamera reached out with her good arm and grabbed hold of
the witch's ankle, then called out to Sophia, "I've got her! I'll
keep her busy. Now run!"

A swift kick ended the act of heroism, and the beast let out a
loud laugh. It pointed at the nun with a smirk as it looked over
to Sophia.

"What is this pathetic waste of flesh to you?"

Suddenly, her voice switched back to Teresa's as she asked,
"Is this bitch your fake mother? You just went out and got some
cheap replacement, huh? Well, that's okay, you don't need this

rip-off anymore." She bent down and grabbed Tamera by the back of her neck. "I'm strong enough to take care of you. Now we can be a family. You don't need this piece of trash anymore!"

"Stop!" Sophia insisted as desperation fluttered through her. She spotted the broken femur and scooped it up, ready to use it as a weapon. "Don't you fucking hurt her!"

"We'll do whatever we want to her, you weak worm! A bastard will not tell me what to do."

Teresa's voice came back once again as she wrapped her fingers around Tamera's throat. "Cover your eyes, sweetie; this is going to get messy."

"Don't do this!" Sophia screamed. "Mom! Don't do this."

The witch's grip around Tamera's throat loosened as a stunned expression crossed Teresa's face. "What...what did you just say? Did...did you just call me mom?"

Sophia had only said that in desperation, but she was relieved that it had worked. She didn't want to become a family with the horrible monster that had caused so much pain in her life, but she could pretend. That seemed to be the witch's only vulnerability.

"That's what you are, aren't you?" Sophia asked as she hid the broken femur behind her back.

"Yes! Yes, of course," Teresa exclaimed with joy.

Sophia took a step forward as she said, "Then you need to let her go." There was hesitation on the witch's face, so she pushed further. "All the killing, it has to stop. If you keep killing, I won't stay. So, show me you can stop. Let her go."

The witch released her grip on Tamera, and she fell to the ground. Sophia took a few steps forward while Teresa eagerly ran over and embraced her.

"Oh, honey," she whispered as tears began to pour. "I've thought about this moment for so long. More than anything, the thought of being with you kept me going." Teresa hugged her daughter a little tighter. "I never wanted to give you up, but I had to. I was so weak after I gave birth, there was no way I could raise you. The thing inside of me, it kept me alive in the dirt. It gave me just enough power to survive and give birth to you, but that was it. I used every ounce of my strength to get you to that orphanage. I could barely walk or move after that. It killed me inside to give you up, but there was no way I was going to give you what you needed."

"What about after you woke up?" Sophia asked.

"Huh?"

She carefully moved the femur, so it was down by her side as she asked, "After you woke up from your long nap, why didn't you come get me?"

"I was still too weak," Teresa answered as she pulled back a bit to look at her daughter's face. "I needed more time..."

She was interrupted by Sophia stabbing the femur into her side. The witch let out a shriek as the bone was twisted around in the wound.

"You didn't want me. You were too busy eating people to even remember I existed," Sophia snapped.

She let go of the makeshift weapon and scrambled back a few feet just to be safe. The stab didn't hurt Teresa as much as surprised her. She was stunned by it and stumbled back a bit, not looking where she was going. Her feet landed in the fire, and the burning sensation sent waves of unpleasant memories spiking across her brain.

"No! No! No!" she screamed as she began flailing about in a panic.

Sophia seized the opportunity and grabbed the largest bone she could find, then used it as a makeshift bat, smacking it against the back of the witch's skull. As Teresa lay on the ground, she pulled the femur free, then stabbed it into the side of the murderer's burnt neck.

"W-Why?" Teresa gasped as blood pulled from the new wound.

Sophia ripped the femur free and screamed, "Because you killed the love of my life, you bitch!" She stabbed the witch in the abdomen. "You're a fucking murderer! That's all you are!"

A barrage of stabs then ensued while Tamera struggled to stand up using only one arm. By the time she had hobbled over to stop Sophia, blood and tissue covered the floor around the eviscerated corpse.

She placed a gentle hand on her adopted daughter's shoulder and said, "She's dead. You did it."

Sophia got to her feet, breathing heavily. She stared down at the mutilated body and emotionlessly repeated, "She's dead."

"Yeah, yeah, she is. It's over now, so let's go home," Tamera said as she turned to the entrance of the cave.

"No, it's not over," Sophia insisted with a hardened look on her face. "There's too much trauma. It will never be over."

Tamera shook her head. "You've been through a lot, but we can get through it. It will take time, but this too will pass."

"No, it won't." Sophia gestured to Teresa. "She never recovered from it, and neither did Shallowroot. Everyone there is scarred by it, they can't move past it. Something like this, it's too much to come back from. I just stabbed my biological mother because she ate the love of my life. You don't recover from that." She swallowed hard. "It's not like I can just go back and pretend everything is okay. The townsfolk hate me. I'm the embodiment of their trauma. As long as I'm here, they will never heal."

"You don't know that."

"You're right," Sophia said in agreement. "That's not for me to decide." She took the bloodied femur and placed it into Tamera's hand, and the two locked gazes. "You decide."

About the Author

Radar DeBoard

Radar DeBoard is just a simple horror writer, living in the bleak state of Kansas. Recently, he has grown weary of the limitations of his craft when it comes to scares. Sure, he has terrified many thanks to having four published books to his name as well as being featured in dozens of horror anthologies, but the fear from those stories wears off.

He wishes to create something so horrific that it lingers in the reader's mind for years to come. Creating something of such unfathomable terror would cement him in the brains of those who purchase his books. Plus, it would be as if he left a piece of himself in each copy of his work. A small bit of himself that can grow and watch, waiting for the right time to deliver a final fright.

DREAMWHISPERS by M Ennenbach
CREMATED REMAINS by M Ennenbach
CUCKOO by M Ennenbach
OLD TOO SOON by Brian Bowyer
BLACKOUT: MICROPOETRY by Brian Bowyer
INNOCENCE ENDS by Nikolas P. Robinson
HAVE A BLAST by Nikolas P. Robinson
COME OUT & PLAY by Patrick Tumblety
ROADS TO RUIN by Brian Bowyer
SUBJECT A by M Ennenbach
OIOS LYKOS by M Ennenbach
STORYSLAVE by Brian Bowyer
VERUM MALUM by Michael R. Collins
PENNYROYAL TEA by Aaron Lebold
THE SHERIFF OF SALEM by Aaron Lebold
GENOCIDE by Aaron Lebold
QUARANTINE by Aaron Lebold
BLASPHEMY by Aaron Lebold
SLENDER BONES IN SACRED SOIL by Fredrick Niles
THIS IS HOW A VILLAIN IS MADE by Amanda Headlee
COFFEE SHOP by Aaron Lebold
ONE FRIGHT ONLY by Patrick Tumblety
WHITE FLIGHT by Peter O'Keefe
BADLANDS by Jason Nickey

Order signed copies and limited-edition hardcovers from the shop:
https://www.uncomfortablydark.com/shop

Join our Patreon for free books, merch, and more!
https://www.patreon.com/user/membership?u=12231330&view
_as=patron